REAL GIRL

www.penguin.co.uk

Real Girl

MUTYA BUENA

bantam

TRANSWORLD PUBLISHERS

UK | USA | Canada | Ireland | Australia
India | New Zealand | South Africa

Transworld is part of the Penguin Random House group of companies
whose addresses can be found at global.penguinrandomhouse.com.

Penguin Random House UK, One Embassy Gardens,
8 Viaduct Gardens, London SW11 7BW

penguin.co.uk

Penguin
Random House
UK

First published in Great Britain in 2025 by Bantam
an imprint of Transworld Publishers

001

Typeset in 12/16pt Minion Pro by Jouve (UK), Milton Keynes
Printed and bound in Great Britain by Clays Ltd, Elcograf S.p.A.

The authorized representative in the EEA is Penguin Random House Ireland,
Morrison Chambers, 32 Nassau Street, Dublin D02 YH68.

A CIP catalogue record for this book is available from the British Library

ISBN: 9780857506849

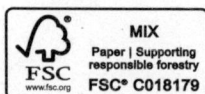

Dedicated to my loved ones and my princess

ONE

I WAS THE UNEXPECTED GIRL. Before I arrived in the world, my mum and dad only had boys – four in all. Now here I was, Rosa Isabel Buena – born on 21 May 1985 and nicknamed 'Mutya', which means Princess Pearl in my dad's native Filipino. The nickname stuck because I was my dad's princess, and he never called me anything else. In school, everyone called me Rosa, but at home, it was always Mutya. Looking back, it's funny to think of how embarrassed I'd get when my parents called me Mutya in front of my school friends. They'd screw up their faces, all confused, and say, 'Who's Mutya?' and I'd have to explain, red-faced and mortified, not knowing that one day it would be the name the world knew me by. Eventually, I got over that embarrassment and when it came to choosing a stage name a few years later, I went with Mutya because it felt unusual and unique. Now, the only people who call me Rosa are the ones who have known me for a hundred years.

I was born into a rowdy household and quickly learned to fight back hard and hold my own. My brothers were those typical naughty boys, always out having fun and getting into mischief. I'm not going to lie; having four older brothers could be difficult at times. Being the only girl meant I had to grow up fast and stay strong if I wanted to keep up with them. I probably have the strength and personality I've got because of it.

They all had very different personalities. Charlie, the eldest, was always the toughest on me. He was the one that ruled the roost and whose permission I often had to ask to do anything – especially when I got older and it came to boys and going out. I suppose it was his way of showing he cared.

We all had a lot of fun together, but that's not to say that being the baby sister wasn't painful at times. On one occasion, I got caught in the middle of a fight between my brothers Charlie and Danny. In a rare occurrence, my mum and dad had popped across the road to the pub with my auntie, so my older siblings were left in charge. During the scrap, I somehow got shoved into the ladder of their bunkbeds and cut my ear badly. The scar from it is still there, and mirrors a scar my dad has in the very same place on the same ear. My brothers fought so much that, in the end, my dad set up a little boxing ring in the smaller bedroom, so they could play fight and safely let off steam under his supervision.

The bunkbed incident wasn't the only pain I suffered as a little sister either. Our family home had a big wooden door leading to the kitchen, which didn't have a handle so was tricky to open. My brother Danny – who's five years older than me – often used my head as the door-opener, pushing it against the wood to shove it open. I guess you could say Danny and I had a classic love–hate sibling relationship. As mean as he was to me sometimes, I knew he cared about me, and I always tried to give as good as I got. Mostly I got away with it, and as much as we butted heads, sometimes literally, Danny would always be the one I sang duets with, performing in Filipino music shows as we got older.

Kris, closest to me in age, was the sweet-boy. He was a charmer, a heartbreaker, and everyone fancied him. Roberto, the third oldest, was also very popular with the girls. Down the line, he was the one all my school friends would moon over when they came to visit. In fact, sometimes, they only came to visit so they could check out one of my brothers, which was a constant source of annoyance for me.

I think I learned a fair bit about boys growing up with so many around me. I figured out how their brains worked, and paid attention to how they acted around their girlfriends. They could be overbearing at times, but it was comforting knowing they were always there. I always felt safe and protected.

After me came three more girls, followed by another boy – so there were nine of us altogether: from the top, Charlie, born in 1978; Danniello (Danny), born in 1980; Eustaquio Roberto, named after my dad and born in 1981; and Kris, born in 1983. Then, after me, Maya, born 1986; Mariatheresa Ligaya, born 1990; Dalisay Michelle, born 1992; and finally, Michael Bayani, born in 1994. He's the baby, now aged thirty.

I did some research into ancestry and the Spanish element to our names, and found out it comes from the colonization of the Philippines by Spain in the 1800s. A lot of Filipinos have Spanish surnames because at one point the governor decreed that all inhabitants of the Philippines should adopt Spanish or Westernized last names. Turns out, my family is a mix of Spanish and Chinese – my dad's mum was from Spanish heritage, while his grandfather was Chinese.

My closest-in-age sister, Maya, passed away when she was a baby. She would have been about a year younger than me. I don't know the exact details of what happened, just that my mum was very ill during her labour. In the end, Maya died just a few hours after she was born.

Despite her short time in the world, Maya has always been

very much seen as part of our family. Mum and Dad have always kept her ashes at home. When I was little, Mum would say, 'Give your sister a kiss and say good morning' each day when I got up, and I'd kiss the little box containing her ashes. It might sound weird to others, but it felt very natural to us. On her birthday and Christmas, we would bring her out and light candles for her.

Sometimes when my school friends came over, they would stare at the container on the kitchen table and ask, 'What is that?'

'Oh, that's my sister Maya,' I'd say, like it was no big deal having someone's ashes where we ate our breakfast.

I always feel sad when I think about what it would've been like to grow up with a sister much closer in age to me. My next sister after Maya is five years younger than me, so there's quite a gap. I always wonder what she would look like now and how alike we might be. Mum says when Maya was born, she looked exactly the same as I did as a newborn. Maybe she would've been a mini-me. Would we be extra close and insep-arable, or competitive and tearing each other's hair out? There are so many questions that I'll never have an answer to. On the third Sugababes album, *Three*, I wrote a song called 'Maya', dedicated to my little sister. It was a soft, soulful lullaby set to the sound of a heartbeat.

Years later, after my grandad passed away, we had two sets of ashes sitting side by side. At one point, I had them set up in a corner by my front door, surrounded by candles. Friends who came over would take one look at it and wonder what the hell it was, my little shrine, but I didn't care. The idea that my sister and grandfather were with me in my home felt comfort-ing to me.

Our enormous, ever-expanding family all lived in a three-bedroom flat in Kingsbury, north-west London. It was madness, and we were always in each other's way, but somehow we made it work. There was a lot of noise, a lot of music, and even more food.

When I think of our family home back then, my mind goes straight to the food. Mum was quite a simple cook, so dinner would often be fish fingers, baked beans, fish and chips or burgers, but there was always rice cooking in the rice pot – every day. My dad brought the Filipino flavours to the household, frying chicken adobo – or some other form of Filipino chicken or meat dish – and filling the house with the smell of vinegar, soy sauce and garlic.

Sometimes, Mum and Dad would disappear in the middle of the night while we were all sleeping. I'd hear the door latch click and wonder where they were going, but they never told me. It was years before I found out, opening the fridge one morning to find a whole pig's head staring back at me. It gave me a scare that first time, but that's when I realized where they'd been sneaking off to in the early hours – the fresh meat market. Not that there was much I wanted to eat in there – giblets? Offal? No, thank you very much! Dad may not have been living in the Philippines, but he'd certainly created his own little corner of it in our flat in north-west London.

For me that was only ever a good thing, knowing what my roots were and where our family had originated from. Having people from the Filipino community around me meant that I was always exposed to the culture, and I'm grateful for that.

That sense of family and culture is something I've held on to. I eat the food of the country and listen to the music because it grounds me. It's something I've tried to pass on to my daughter.

I want her to know the importance of it too, because I feel like my best childhood moments were always the times when I was immersed in my culture. It's beautiful to have grown up in a place like that.

As you can imagine, things tended to be chaotic in the Buena house. This only got worse as the family continued to expand and my older brothers started to bring their girlfriends round. On top of that, we also had so many animals on the go. Growing up, I had guinea pigs, hamsters, rabbits, cats and fish, and my brothers sometimes kept lizards and weird-coloured frogs.

It was madness, but I loved it, and special occasions like Christmas were always amazing. Mum would cover every available space in tinsel, and we'd always have a tree, even though there wasn't really enough room for one. It always amazed me how many people we managed to get around a table for Christmas dinner, all crammed in like sardines.

Generally, it all worked because we are a loving family, but you would have often heard the cry of teenage Mutya telling my little sisters not to touch my stuff, and when my brothers got into an argument, there was no escape. That was the worst in a tiny flat: the screaming and shouting bouncing off every wall, with nowhere to hide from it.

Being the only girl for a while meant that I at least had my own bedroom when I was little, while my brothers shared the other. Eventually, as my younger sisters came along, I had to share with them, but by then, the boys were older and moving out with their various partners so it all balanced out. I remember seeing a lot of girlfriends come and go while I was growing up, including the women some of them are still with. This was something we all got used to very quickly, with my sisters and I seeing them as part of the family.

At one point, Mum and Dad moved into the living room when my eldest brother moved back in with his girlfriend, and eventually, when they had kids of their own, we all lived together under one roof. And yes, sharing limited space sometimes meant fights and arguments, but generally, as crowded as it was, these were fun and happy times.

Our home always felt warm and welcoming, so there was a constant stream of visitors; friends who'd talk, laugh and eat together while my dad entertained. Mum would sit chatting and smoking, while Dad would have a whisky or two with his mates. I must have met and interacted with so many different people as a child, I guess it's no surprise I've never really been a shy adult.

Mum was a chatterbox, so if we ever came into the house and didn't see her straight away, we knew she'd be in the kitchen, puffing on a cigarette as always and nattering to someone, whether that be a neighbour, a friend or one of my brothers' girlfriends. She loved to talk, so there'd often be four or five people crammed into our tiny kitchen while she held court. She was very sociable and always young in heart and mind. Dad, meanwhile, preferred heading out to the bookies for a flutter to get a break from all the noise.

'I'm going to the office,' he'd say, and we all knew what that meant.

There was a pub opposite our estate where the grown-ups would regularly hang out and play pool. Quite often, a gang of them would come back to the house with Mum and Dad after closing, and the place would be filled with singing, dancing and joy. The lights were always on and there was always food and music.

Despite this rowdy existence, our house was always clean and well organized. Mum was extremely houseproud and had this crazy habit of cleaning at odd times of the night. She'd sometimes wake up at four a.m., get the mop and bucket out of the cupboard, and off she'd go. It wouldn't have been so bad if she was just quietly mopping the floor while we all slept; it was the blasting soundtrack of Fleetwood Mac that went along with it that was the problem. If Mum was up doing her early-hours housework, we were all awake! I'd sit up in bed, music blaring through the wall, the smell of bleach creeping under the door, and think, *Oh my god, she's at it again!* She was always cleaning or rearranging something. We lived in a house where you never knew where to find a fucking teaspoon because they were never in the place you last saw them. The layout of the flat was constantly changing.

That's the thing I've inherited from my mum: the ability to rearrange furniture at a moment's notice. You could walk into my living room one day and things would be a certain way, and come back the next day and not know where the hell you were. It drives my daughter mad!

My dad first came to the UK in his teens but had returned to the Philippines to join the army. Eventually, he came back to England, and that's when he met Mum, an east London girl born and bred in Whitechapel.

All of Dad's family were military-based. His father was a high-ranking officer, and he and my grandma lived in a house that was right opposite the army base. His brothers had been in the Filipino army too, and Dad's older brother was tragically killed during military exercises in Manila – he was shot in the eye.

Dad's military background meant that he could sometimes be strict with us kids. I've even got photos of us all saluting him. He wasn't mean, but he kept us all in line. In our house there was no such thing as crying. If I ever did cry, I'd better have a bloody good reason. Looking back, I realize that was just how he was brought up, but there were definitely times we wished he would loosen up a bit. On the flip side of that, I got to experience a much softer side of him than the others. I was his first baby girl and his princess, after all, so I definitely got away with a few things that my brothers didn't!

My mum was different. She wasn't as strict and was more likely than my dad to give in when we begged for sweets. I have vivid memories of hounding her at what we called the cake shops in my primary school. These were days when kids would bring in cakes baked by someone in the family, to sell to their friends.

I was always on at my mum on those days. 'Mum, please can I have some money to buy a cake?'

Back then, they were selling for ten or twenty pence each, but with so many of us in the family, Mum couldn't always afford to dole out cash to satisfy my sweet tooth. I was most appreciative of the days when she could.

Mum is a sweetheart, but she could be fiery if you got on her bad side. She was a pale-skinned redhead and proper cockney, even though her family were originally from Ireland. When I was little and out with my parents, Filipino people often thought Mum was my nanny or childminder. And everyone said I looked like my dad. It was quite unusual to see a white lady with a Filipino man; it was more common the other way around, so people in the community assumed my dad hired her to look after me. Sometimes, people didn't even acknowledge her when we stood side by side because we looked so different. Mum would always feel very hurt by this and was quite vocal when someone suggested that I wasn't her daughter.

'I'm not her fucking nanny, I'm her mum,' she'd say.

Eventually, people got to know, accept and love her for who she was, but it took a while. She was most definitely a hot mamma back in the day too. She never left the house in anything other than a mini-skirt. It didn't matter what the weather was; she'd be in a Lycra mini, with her make-up done and her hair perfectly styled – straightened or permed, and, as the years went on, dyed. She'd never let her grey show if she could help it, and I say, good for her.

I will never forget the day when she finally started wearing leggings instead of the short skirts.

'What is this?' I said. 'You must be getting older!'

Mum has such a beautiful, bubbly personality and is always fun. She's always been one of the girls, and to this day if I'm going out for the night with my girlfriends, I'll bring my mum along with me. She's always been my saviour, the person I've been able to be most honest with. She knows everything about me, and if anyone ever thinks they have juicy information to spill to her, I'd never worry. Trust me, she already knows that shit.

My friends all love her too. In fact, there have been many times over the years when I wasn't around but my girlfriends would still go hang out with Mum, enjoy a good chat with her, as well as a cup of tea and a fag. That's how it was where we lived. People came and went like family. Our estate, Piper's Green, was a real little community, and on sunny summer days, all the mums would be outside with their cuppas, puffing on their ciggies, chatting about everything and everyone. Meanwhile, us kids would be running around or riding our bikes up and down the estate or around the block. The only thing that would stop us in our tracks was the familiar sound of the ice-cream van pulling up. The twinkly music echoing around the flats would have us all running towards it, pestering our mums for money to buy something. On the hottest days, someone would drag out a paddling pool to the grassy patch in the middle of the estate and fill it with water so we could all splash about in it. I sometimes think that kind of thing is missing these days; that close community where kids could go knock on a neighbour's door and ask if their mates were allowed to come out to play, always in and out of one another's houses, with a friend's parent asking, 'Do you want to stay for dinner?'

That's how it was for us as children. We knew everybody on the estate, and all the mums and dads looked out for each other's kids. I was always very proud of coming from Piper's Green. In fact, for one Sugababes behind-the-scenes shoot back in the day, I took an entire camera crew there to show it off.

TWO

THERE WERE SO MANY DIFFERENT types of music that filled our house when I was growing up. Mum loved to sing, and she listened to Fleetwood Mac, T. Rex and the Carpenters, while my dad was into Guns N' Roses and Bon Jovi. Mum also loved reggae and Motown, and Dad even liked a bit of heavy metal, so I don't think there was any genre of music I wasn't exposed to in one way or another.

I was into classic nineties pop and R&B, and that has stayed with me. When I was very young, in the eighties, I was obsessed with New Kids On The Block. My brothers bought me my first concert videotape, which featured one of their major tours, and I had posters of them all over my bedroom. From New Kids, going into the next decade, I moved on to N-Sync, Backstreet Boys, Charles and Eddie, plus R&B acts like SWV, Xscape, Monica, Brandy and Aaliyah. On the other side of the coin, I loved Frank Sinatra, Bread and Barbra Streisand. My listening habits were broad because I'd been exposed to many different genres of music via my parents. I also loved garage because my brother Charlie was a DJ on a few of the pirate radio stations, and that's what he liked to play. My other brother Danny was more into drum 'n' bass and jungle, so I was exposed to that too, and there was also a lot of good American hip-hop around at that time. With such varying tastes, there was often music of all sorts blaring out of every room at the same time, all fighting for a place. All of those musical vibes and influences were swirling around me at every moment of every day, and I soaked them all up. As different as it all was, it all made sense to me, and taste-wise, I'm still pretty much rooted in that era to this day. I can't seem to move away from it. I guess some people would say I'm stuck in my ways, but it's just what I love.

We didn't just listen to music in our house; we played it too. As far back as I can remember, my dad always played guitar. As well as Mum's noisy night-time cleaning, another soundtrack to the early hours would be Dad strumming away, singing at the top of his voice as we all tried to sleep. I can't count the number of times I drifted off to the sound of my dad's singing coming from the living room. To be honest, it's a wonder we got any shut-eye at all. He also had a keyboard, and at one point he even brought a drumkit home.

He had this pile of music books like you wouldn't believe – thick notebooks full of songs, sheet music and lyrics. Most nights he'd flick through these, looking for songs for us to sing together. 'Tie A Yellow Ribbon Round The Ole Oak Tree' was one I remember well, plus classics by the Jackson 5 and Fleetwood Mac, for my mum. Dad would gather me and my older brothers around him, and we'd all sit down and sing together in the living room. I would sing 'Crazy' by Patsy Cline, 'Evergreen' by Barbra Streisand, and always a bit of Whitney to finish things off! We were all musical to certain degrees, and in truth, I think Dad secretly hoped we might end up becoming an entire family of performers – like the Jackson 5 or the Osmonds.

Looking back now, it seems like a weird thing to do, all sitting down to sing together like that family from *The Sound of Music* – it's not what most families would do of an evening – but

there's something warm and wonderful about the memory of
it. I'm also very grateful to my dad for giving me that focus
on music, making sure I sang every day and had new songs
to learn after school and before bedtime, even though sometimes I'd have preferred to be running around outside with my
friends. It's almost as if he knew that was the road I should
be taking, even before I did. I don't think I'd necessarily have
gone down the path towards music if Dad hadn't steered me in
that direction. There are so many things that might never have
happened if he hadn't. I had a happy childhood, and my dad
bringing so much music into our lives was a big part of that.
When I think back, I feel so much nostalgia for it – the record
player was always spinning, and my dad would be strumming
his guitar, while Mum sat and watched him adoringly. She
always called him her Superman. They were so in love, and
still are to this day.

With and without my brothers, I'd been singing with my dad
for quite some time when he put me forward for the Little Miss
Philippines pageant. It was a children's beauty pageant which
included a talent section, and he was sure I'd do well. The con-
test was held in Romney Marsh in Kent, and there I was, aged
seven, wearing a big old frilly dress with 'Miss Visayas' written
across my sash. Visayas is the name of a group of islands in the
Philippines where my family came from. The dress was pretty
horrendous, to be honest, with huge puffy shoulders and ruf-
fles for days. Not my style at all, but that's what everybody wore.
I remember being very nervous that first time. I never thought
of myself as the classic 'pretty little girl', so seeing all these cute
olive-skinned girls lining up on stage put me on edge. A lot of
them were full Filipino too, while I was only half and much

paler. I ended up making some very good friends from those kinds of competitions, but that first one, I didn't know anyone and felt like I stuck out like a frilly sore thumb.

As well as looking pretty, all the contestants were expected to know certain facts about the Philippines, and be able to answer questions on the subject. I'd studied hard beforehand, so when we were asked how many islands there were in total, I knew the answer was 7,641, and I've never forgotten it. I also had to learn the country's national anthem, which my dad had to sit me down and teach me to sing in his native language. Looking back, I wished I'd learned even more Tagalog. If my dad had taught us his native language, think of the fun my sisters and I could have had gossiping about people in a foreign tongue they couldn't understand. These days, being around the community as long as I have, I know a fair bit of the lingo, but it's more a case of me understanding rather than speaking it.

For the pageant, each contestant was expected to do something impressive for the talent section, so, of course, I sang for the judges. It was my first time singing for anyone other than my family. I can't remember the song (it might have been Patsy Cline's 'Crazy') but my voice was certainly the thing that made people sit up and take notice. I might not have been as cute and well turned out as some of the other girls, but I'd definitely earned my place in the competition. In the end, I got the runner-up prize, and afterwards word began to spread about my singing ability. Suddenly, at the grand old age of seven, I found myself in demand. People would call my dad and ask if I could perform at their parties and events – weddings, birthdays, even funerals. I had it all coming at me, and I mostly enjoyed it because I was never bored; I was always getting invited somewhere to do something. In any case, I was too young to have a say in the matter anyway. I'd hear my dad talking on the phone in Tagalog or Bisayan, and if the word 'Mutya' jumped out of the conversation, I knew I'd booked a gig, whatever it was. I felt a bit like a human karaoke machine, but there were benefits. I remember one party, I was singing my heart out while watching three or four pint glasses being passed around, into which people were putting money. I don't remember what the event was, but most of the time Filipinos don't need an excuse to throw a party, anyway. We love a function, whether it's celebrating someone recovering from an illness or getting a new job.

At the end of the night, after I'd finished my last song, the glasses, now heavy with coins and notes, were presented to me. I hadn't gone there to get paid; I'd simply gone to perform, and get my fill of free food and juice, so this was a real bonus. Filipinos are always very generous, and after that night, I often found myself leaving these gigs with cash in my pocket. I thought I was the shit! I felt special.

In the early days, Dad would record instrumental backing tracks on to cassette tapes, and I would sing over those, or sometimes he would accompany me on the guitar. Eventually, as karaoke became more and more widespread, most people had a machine I could use, and if they didn't, we would bring our own one along.

I remember moaning about doing it a few times, feeling overexposed as the regular party singer in our community. Surely people were getting tired of seeing my face? Strangely, that never seemed to be the case. Wherever I performed, I was fed well and made to feel very welcome. Because my dad knew so many people within the community, I always felt comfortable doing what I was doing. Everyone felt like family, even though these were often celebrations that had nothing to do with me. Those events performing for my community really were the start of my career, and I loved it.

There is something about Filipino people and music. Music and singing are a huge and important part of the culture; it's like we're deeply connected to it somehow. If you ever visit the Philippines, you'll see that almost every house has a karaoke machine. They're almost as common as a fridge or washing machine. If you were to go to an electrical store to buy a TV, you'd see people there testing out the microphones and sound systems on the karaoke machines, and not just with a few words; we're talking a full-out performance with crowds of people drifting in off the street to watch. It would be like walking into your local branch of Currys in the UK and seeing people belt out an entire set of full-blown ballads in the middle of the store, one after the other. It happens all the time, and these days you can see it all over TikTok. The funny thing is, looking at it on my phone, it seems crazy, watching people singing their hearts out surrounded by toasters and microwaves, but when I see it happen in real life, it feels perfectly normal.

I don't know where this affinity with music comes from, but I think it's because we're such a happy community. Music has always been something that brings people together and that we can enjoy as a group. It's not about making money or doing it professionally: people sing because they find joy in doing it. It's not just singing, either. My dad plays six or seven different types of guitar, and most of his family, like many Filipinos, play an instrument of some sort.

And of course, where there's music, there's dancing. The people who organized the Little Miss Philippines pageant also ran a weekend stage school, Europhil, which had Filipino dance classes. I spent most weekends there, learning some of the language and the traditional dances, as well as ballet, tap, street and even Hawaiian and Tahitian dance. I loved all the different types of dancing, but I really got into the traditional Philippine folk dances and became very good at them. I wasn't really bothered about learning Tagalog at the time, and I don't think Dad was that bothered either. For me, and for my parents, it was just important to have something outside of school to focus on. I think by the time I joined Europhil, Mum and Dad could both see that I was heading in the direction of being a performer of some kind, and that this was the perfect outlet. I enjoyed the discipline of having dances to learn and a schedule to stick to. It served me well in later life, as these days I always like to be on time if not early for everything.

One of the traditional folk dances I learned back then is called Tinikling, which involves two or more people tapping and sliding bamboo poles on the ground. Meanwhile, dancers step over and dance in and out of the poles. Another one was the candle dance, known as Pandanggo, where you dance with candles in glass jars balanced on your head and outstretched palms. This one involves lots of difficult tricks, intricate moves and dropping down to the floor, all without letting the candles fall. They came very naturally to me, and I ended up being one of the most prominent dancers in the school.

Dancing took up my time and focus, and I loved it. I went to primary school during the week, but I was living for the moment when I could put on my leggings and big socks, dance the weekend away and work my fabulous calves! As well as the traditional dance, I also loved ballet, and got a real kick from working my way up through all the grades.

When I was about nine or ten, I was asked to join a dance group called Pipa, who were a professional touring company. The dancers in that group were all a bit older than me; most of them were older teenagers. With Pipa, I travelled all around Europe dancing and singing in big shows for various Filipino communities. On these trips, Mum came with me as my chaperone.

For the performances, there were certain songs we did every night. We always opened with Sister Sledge's 'We Are Family', and ended with Starship's 'Nothing's Gonna Stop Us Now'. The middle section changed show to show. There were solo songs, a few duets and lots of traditional music, as well as all the folk dancing that was our speciality. It was all hugely entertaining; a real theatrical experience with full hair, make-up and costume.

Those trips to Europe with Pipa were a ball of fun, and I got to meet so many people from the Filipino community in each new country, sampling all the variations of the food and culture. I even loved the travel, feeling all grown up, sitting at the back of the plane with the adults smoking their cigarettes – it feels weird to think of people smoking on a plane now, but back then it was allowed. It was an eye-opening experience for little Mutya, but at the time, I didn't think of it as anything other than a little hobby on the side; something I was lucky enough to do when I wasn't in school. I definitely had a few childhood dreams of becoming a pop star, but I didn't really equate those with what I was doing with Pipa. I certainly couldn't have imagined all the things that would come after it.

I felt quite blessed to be enjoying the experience of foreign travel. Up until then our family holidays had been to places like Bournemouth and other classic seaside spots in the UK; sometimes we went to Butlins if we were really lucky. There were so many of us that holidays abroad weren't always an option for our massive family; it would have just been too expensive. That meant that my little trips with Pipa were my only experiences of other countries, despite not being technically holidays.

That's why it felt huge when, at the age of twelve, I took a trip to the Philippines with my dad to visit our family who lived there. None of my brothers and sisters went with us – it was just him and me. My brothers all desperately wanted to go, but because money was tight, there was no way we would all be able to make the trip. Being Daddy's Princess and the performer in the family, I guess I got preferential treatment. I'd been performing for and mixing with the Filipino community for some time by then and I think Dad wanted me to see and experience more of his homeland.

Leading up to the trip, I'd been on at Mum to let me get my hair cut. At the time, it was dead straight and down past my bum, but I wanted the Jennifer Aniston layered look that a lot of the girls in my school were getting. My parents were having none of it, but still, I'd beg.

'Mum, please let me get the Jennifer haircut!'

'You're not cutting your hair, Mutya,' she would reply repeatedly.

She always loved styling my long hair, brushing it or plaiting it before bed, and hated the idea of me getting it chopped off. I think, in her eyes, my long hair somehow kept me young. Her little girl!

I was envious of the other girls at school, with bouncy layers and highlights. There was no way I was going to be allowed to have dye anywhere near my head, so one of my school friends made a suggestion before I left for the Philippines: 'Why don't you put some Sun-In on your hair and let it lighten naturally while you're out there?'

Sun-In was a big thing back in the day, a mix of peroxide and lemon that you sprayed in your hair, so it lightened over time in sunlight. But Mum wouldn't let me do that either.

'No haircutting and no dyeing!'

So, I left the UK with my hair trailing down my back, dead straight with my boring natural colour.

On that trip, I stayed at my lola's house – that's 'grandmother' in my dad's native language – which had four bedrooms. Multiple generations of our family lived under that roof, with one of my dad's brothers and his family occupying each bedroom. One of the main reasons I'd wanted to make the trip was to meet my cousins for the first time. Despite Mum and Dad having four boys, the Buenas are generally a family of females. Even now, with my nineteen nieces and nephews, there are only four boys among them, and it was the same back then in the Philippines. Girls everywhere, and it was so wonderful meeting them all. It's true, there were a few Filipino people back home who I thought of as family, but these were actually my blood relatives, and there was an instant connection. I was a similar age to one of my uncle's girls, so it was easy to find common ground between us, although I was aware of how much stricter their upbringing was compared to mine. Their parents were a lot tougher on them generally. My uncles all seemed to have that military mindset, so that's how they tried to keep everyone in line. If my cousins were told to do something by their parents, they did it. No messing. Despite these differences, and me bringing my Western ways to their doorstep, we all got along very well, and I felt very happy to be spending time with them.

It was a fun, exciting trip with my senses on overload, taking in the country's beautiful sights, sounds and culture – some of them more unusual than I was used to in the community at home. Back then, cockfighting was still a thing, and there were these crazy festivals with horses galloping around all over the place. Everything felt brighter, louder, crazier than I was used to. The thing I noticed the most was how close the community was and how 'as one' and open the people were. During celebrations, whether it be Christmas, Easter or just somebody's birthday, if the door of a house was open, you were welcome to go inside and eat something. It didn't matter if you knew the family who lived there or not. My lola's house always seemed to have an open door. Everyone knew everyone, so people would be swanning in unannounced all the time, and they were always welcomed. The funny thing about meeting all those different people was that, mostly, they didn't think of me as Filipino.

'Where are you from?' people often asked me, and I'd always feel slightly insulted. I wanted to be thought of as one of them, but they could tell the difference.

At least there wasn't too much of a language barrier between us. Almost everyone in the Philippines speaks English, as it's an official language of the country.

My biggest culture shock came when I was visiting one of my cousins who lived elsewhere. My dad suggested I go up to her room while he caught up with his brother. When I walked into her bedroom, I noticed an opening in the roof, and I was quite taken aback. *What the hell did she do when it rained?* I wondered. Before I could finish the thought or ask the question, my cousin held up her hand.

'Just stay there,' she said, with a weird look in her eye.

I stopped in my tracks just as a monkey on a long leash came flying through the hole in her roof, landing directly in front of me. She had a fucking monkey in her room, and it wasn't a cute, friendly type of monkey either – quite vicious-looking in fact – although it seemed to like her. Who the hell has a wild monkey in their bedroom? I know I had a lot of pets, but this seemed to take it a bit too far. I'd never seen anything like it, outside of the Tarzan movies. Needless to say, I stood very still and didn't stay long.

As I mentioned, there are 7,641 islands in the Philippines, and we were in the Bohol province, which has many gorgeous white-sand beaches and resorts, as well as the Chocolate Hills – a huge range of green, dome-shaped hills that turn chocolate brown in the dry season and are a big tourist attraction. I felt so lucky to be from such a beautiful country where everything felt so clean and fresh. My cousins had me climbing coconut trees, or out on a boat catching fish for dinner. And there was singing everywhere. Every household seemed to be filled with the sound of music and karaoke. It was a beautiful thing.

At one point during the trip, I told my dad, 'This will be where I live one day. This will be home.'

That hasn't ended up being the case, but I am planning a trip there very soon, my first in six or seven years.

My dad was a different man in the Philippines. He was more laid-back in his old stomping ground, and was less strict with me because of it. This gave me a newfound freedom, and I was determined to make the most of it and rebel. It didn't take long before I started getting up to no good. Starting strong, I got my cousins into trouble almost immediately, persuading them to go out to a local nightclub with me. Let's not forget, the drinking age is eighteen in the Philippines, just like in the UK, and I was twelve, my cousins around the same age – one a bit older, one a bit younger. In my defence, I did at least ask my dad first.

'Ooh, I don't know about that,' Dad said, shaking his head. 'Your cousins are going to have to ask their dad, and I'm not sure he'll be too pleased. You can go, though. Go out and enjoy yourself.'

I was quite surprised my dad was so relaxed about me going, but I knew it wasn't going to be as easy getting my uncle to say yes. Like all my dad's brothers, he was very strict. There was no point in even trying to get permission, so, in the end, I convinced my cousins to go without it. I'd been to a few under-eighteen raves back home by then, so it didn't seem like a big deal to me.

When we got to the club, I shouldn't have been surprised to find that my dad and another of his brothers had turned up on motorbikes and parked themselves outside, just to make sure we were OK. No wonder he'd let me go so easily! Thankfully, knowing how hot-headed my cousins' dad was, his brothers didn't tell him we were going.

Inside the club, we had a great time. I was really into the music. It was 1997, the year of Usher's album *My Way* and the single from it, 'You Make Me Wanna . . .', which I listened to daily on my Walkman as I headed to the beach. That and the Backstreet Boys' *Backstreet's Back* album. Even now, when I hear those tunes, I'm right back on the beach with my cousins.

Everyone in the club was dancing to 'Backstreet's Back' and 'All I Have To Give'. This was a completely new experience for my cousins, so they were living their best life and not thinking about the consequences.

When we eventually got back from the club, my uncle was waiting for us in the kitchen and all hell broke loose. Their dad went mad, and they got into deep shit. Meanwhile, my dad gave me a stern, disappointed look.

'This is what happens when you don't listen,' he said. 'They can't do the stuff you can.'

I did notice a tiny smile cross his mouth. I think, secretly, he found the whole thing quite funny.

That night could've ended in disaster, but instead it left me with a taste for rebellion. A few days after the incident with my cousins, I started to think about what else I could try to get away with. What about the hair? Dare I even ask? Yes, of course I dared.

'Dad, I'm really, really hot,' I complained. 'Can I cut my hair?'

He eyed me suspiciously. 'Mmm. I'm not sure that's a good idea.'

'But Dad, my neck is sweating and I can't put my hair up; it's too long.'

'Mutya, you're gonna get me killed by your mum.'

'Dad, pleeaaase!'

Princess Pearl wins again. I'll always remember our trip to the hair salon. I was so excited about what was about to happen, not quite believing I'd finally won that battle. I left the salon with a smart, stylish bob and I'd never felt more grown up and glamorous. Despite speaking to Mum on the phone during our trip, neither me nor my dad said anything about my haircut. We wanted to put off the argument for as long as possible. When we eventually got home and walked through the front door, we got what was coming for us.

'Mutya, what the fuck did you do?' She was furious and devastated.

'Dad let me cut it because it was so hot,' I said, immediately putting it all on him.

'What? She couldn't have just put her hair up?' she yelled at him.

I suppose I could understand where she was coming from. I was her little girl and I'd never cut my hair. It had just grown and grown since I was a baby, so for her, this was a turning point. The first time she had to accept that I was growing up. Meanwhile, Dad was trying to redeem himself, waving a plastic bag around for Mum to see.

'Look, I've still got the hair,' he said. 'I kept it and brought it home.'

'I don't fucking care about hair in a bag!' Mum shouted. 'It should be on her head!'

I felt like I should step in and help poor Dad, so I suggested, 'Perhaps one day I could have it as hair extensions and put it back in.'

Believe it or not, that bag of hair is still around. I saw it not long ago, and the memory of it made me smile.

THREE

I FIRST MET KEISHA AT primary school – she'd joined my class when we were about nine or ten, but she already knew who I was, recognizing me from a TV appearance I'd made a few months earlier.

I'd been on a show called *My Kind of People* hosted by Michael Barrymore, singing and dancing in Whiteley's shopping centre with my class from Europhil. Off the back of that, I was invited to come on to his other big show, *Barrymore*, to sing 'The Greatest Love Of All' and be interviewed by the man himself. I looked super-cute dressed in a flowery skirt and burgundy-coloured top and sat there, happily telling Michael about the long list of household chores I had to do.

Meanwhile, Keisha was at home as the show aired, and her mum called her over to the TV.

'Come and watch this little girl singing,' her mum said.

When Keisha joined my class, she immediately recognized me. Soon after we met, she pretty much kidnapped me and took me to her house, which was just around the corner from mine.

'Mummy, look, it's that girl from the TV show,' she said.

We were friends from that moment on. Keisha had grown up with the same kinds of music as I had, and we bonded fast over our shared love of singing. Once we started, we couldn't be stopped, and sang constantly, all the way through school.

We even sang a duet for the whole year at our school leaving party, where we performed TLC's 'Red Light Special' and the Fugees' 'Killing Me Softly'. We made an amazing duo, so I suppose it was inevitable we'd both end up going to the same secondary school – Kingsbury High.

Outside of school, Keisha always had a separate group of friends who were very different to my mine. My group were the wild ones who hung out on the estate smoking weed – the mischievous ones, out till all hours. In fact, I was probably the quietest one in my friendship group at that time. It was the same with my friendship with Keisha. I was the quiet one, and Keisha the louder personality, though neither of us were particularly naughty or disruptive. I'd say we were both pretty good students – at least in the first year or so.

Keisha was in a different class to me, so I didn't see as much of her as I had in primary school. Sometimes, I'd go round to her house at weekends, chill and listen to music, but most of the time we'd hang out with our own mates outside of the school gates.

I was the tiniest thing in high school, petite with a pear-shaped head. I recently saw some pictures Keisha has of me, and I'm a mouse. Everyone else towered over me back then. Maybe that's why my older brothers were so overprotective of me. They'd all gone to Kingsbury High too, so by the time I got there, everyone knew who I was. I was 'the little sister', and not to be messed with. This was helpful in some ways, but not in others. Sure, it was nice feeling safe from bullying, but at the same time boys were afraid to talk to me in case they got into trouble with my 'crazy' older brothers. Even when they were no longer in school, that protection continued via some of their younger mates who were still there. It was like having the secret service watching over me. When I unwisely dared to ask permission to talk to a boy one day, a couple of my brothers' younger mates got me in a headlock on the floor.

'What the fuck are you doing?' One of them screamed at me. 'What do you mean, you want to talk to him?'

This all happened in front of half the school, so it was pretty embarrassing. After that there was *no way* any boy would come near me.

For the most part, I enjoyed school, but probably for all the wrong reasons. By the time we were twelve, me and my friend Latoya were leaving our houses at seven in the morning, whatever the weather, just so we could sit in the park by our school to chill and smoke cigarettes before class. These were cigarettes we'd stolen from my mum, who, for years, blamed my brothers for nicking her fags. It's only just recently I owned up to it. We'd go into registration stinking of tobacco.

We all used to call Latoya 'Beady', because she wore her hair in single plaits with beads. I can remember her plaits swinging so vividly as we traipsed to the park, cigarettes hidden in our coat pockets. Now, all these years later, I'm godmother to her son, who's the same age as my daughter, Tahlia. We sometimes laugh about the idea of either of them getting out of bed and out of the house by seven a.m. for anything, let alone to hang out in a bloody park. They'd die at the very idea of it!

As time went on, I often found myself in trouble at school, earning myself detentions for whole months at a time. I was always getting into arguments with my best friend, Abigail – it was a real love–hate relationship with us – and those rows would end up landing us in the shit with certain teachers. It was crazy because I loved Abigail but, in that classic teenage way, we were constantly bickering and it drove everyone up the wall. My school uniform was also a point of annoyance for the staff and they'd sigh every time they saw me coming. I'd march into school wearing Spice Girls trainers instead of regulation footwear. On top of that, my skirt would come down to my ankles with the biggest split at the back that went right up to the start of my arse-crack. My girls and I all had different-coloured Puffa jackets we loved wearing – mine was orange, and I'd stolen it from my brother. These jackets came in very handy when we didn't have enough money to pay for our school lunches – normally because we'd spent it all on something else. We'd slink into the canteen where one of us would take a chicken burger, another would get fries and someone else would grab a pudding with custard. We'd hide them in our giant jackets and stroll out like butter wouldn't melt. I'd smile innocently as I walked past other kids and staff who would never have dreamed that I was smuggling custard beneath my very cool orange Puffa.

Quite often, we'd be pulled out of assembly and made to turn around and stand at the back while everyone else sat. This was supposed to be an example to the other children of how not to dress for school, a reminder for them all to always come in wearing the correct uniform, but we thought we were rebels, and secretly enjoyed the attention.

As for lessons, I enjoyed sports but, weirdly, music was my least favourite subject. In fact, I hated everything about it. For me, music had always been about being free and creative. Sitting in a classroom learning about the theory of it, studying sheet music and composition, was something completely alien to me and I found it dry and boring.

The subject I most enjoyed was art. I loved painting and drawing; anything from the human form to landscapes. I was good at it, and it's something I'd have loved to have pursued – but the universe had something else in store for me.

Around that time, my dad was working at an Asian food shop in Acton. Each day, a local man, Ron Tom, would come into the store and they'd chat about this and that, passing the time of day. When they got on to the subject of music one afternoon, Ron told my dad that he'd formed and managed the girl band All Saints. Of course, my proud dad couldn't help but boast about his own daughter's vocal skills. By then, I'd been singing all over Europe with Pipa, becoming quite the little professional. Ron was this loud, crazy guy with a big personality and tons of enthusiasm, and as soon as I was mentioned he suggested my dad bring me over to sing for him.

I'd been singing with Pipa in Rome right before that and I'd arrived back home with a sore throat. Still, when Dad told me that there was a music manager who wanted to hear me sing, I was up for giving it a go. I was a big fan of All Saints and I loved singing, so why not? So, off we went to this complete stranger Ron's house with my mum in tow.

Ron lived in a very nice place, with lots of recording equipment dotted around, and gold and platinum discs on the wall. I was a bit nervous, but not overly so. It was a new experience for me but Ron seemed very friendly, and by then I was fairly confident in my ability. I'd sung for so many people, so this didn't feel all that different. When I think back on it now, I'm not sure I even took it all that seriously, despite knowing Ron's powerful music business connections. Like most things, I took it my stride, never imagining what a pivotal moment in my life this would be.

I started off that day singing a Monica song, and Ron seemed to like it. He then called a good friend of his, Don-E – who's an amazing singer, songwriter and producer – to come down and hear me sing. When Don-E arrived, I sang (or croaked) through a couple more songs, and everyone seemed happy with what I'd done. I left that day without any expectations but soon after, I found myself in the studio with Don-E, recording my own demos, which felt very sudden and exciting. I hadn't signed any contracts; at that stage it was just on the under-standing that if things went well, we would work together. I guess Ron wanted to see how I performed in a studio setting, and whether he felt he could work with me.

Still, these weren't cover versions I was recording, but my own material, written and produced for me by a professional. I remember it being quite nerve-wracking at first. I was expected to deliver vocals on a song that I'd never heard before, because it didn't exist yet! It was something new and fresh that I was helping create. It was the first time I really felt challenged musically, but that being said, I got used to everything pretty quickly and found that I really enjoyed trying different things with my technique and vocal style. Once I'd recorded a few songs, Ron made an announcement. 'I'm putting on an indus-try showcase,' he told us. 'I've got this other girl I'm looking after, Siobhan, and you could both do it.'

'OK, I'm down for that,' I said.

Ron had so many contacts from his years in the business; he knew a lot of successful artists, like Mark Morrison and Gabrielle – artists that I admired and rated – so there were plenty of music industry people there to watch Siobhan and me that day. It was pretty much a full house, and the lead-up was a nail-biting experience. It's not like I wasn't used to performing in front of a crowd, but this was a whole new ball game. It's one thing singing someone else's songs, but something else entirely singing songs that nobody has ever heard before, written especially for me. Up until then, I'd only ever sung for fun, and maybe a few quid and a slice of cake, but suddenly the potential of a career was laid out in front of me.

Siobhan seemed great right from the start – the same lovely person back then that she is now. We clicked straight away. We were there for the same reason and, I guess, both wanted the same thing – for something good and positive to come out of the day. It's crazy to think that we were both barely teenagers, doing this massive thing in front of all Ron's music-biz connections and friends. For the showcase Siobhan and I each sang separately, performing our own material, but it was just the two of us that day. Two thirteen-year-old schoolgirls singing to a room packed full of music industry people.

Not long after that day, Ron suggested that Siobhan and I try recording a song together to see how it sounded. It was one of his wild, out-of-the-box ideas that I got used to over the years, but it was a good one. I couldn't have even dreamed what it would lead to at the time.

When I first started singing with Siobhan, it was a completely new experience for me. Now, not only was I in a professional recording studio, but I was trying to get my voice to sit with another singer's. There was also a sound engineer and a producer present for the first time: people who had certain expectations of how I sang and sounded. I felt quite nervous having only just met Siobhan, but I was determined to give it my best shot, and thankfully, I loved her voice. That day, we recorded a demo and everyone in the room felt it went well and that we sounded good together.

For the next session, I asked Keisha along to the studios with me. It was nothing more than knowing she loved music and might enjoy spending time in a studio environment. We weren't hanging out together much at the time, but we'd never lost that bond of singing together in primary school.

She hadn't been there long when Ron asked her, 'Can you sing too, Keisha?'

Keisha looked a bit uncertain but eventually mumbled a slow 'Yeah!'

'Let's hear you, then,' Ron said, so off she went.

Before long, Ron had all three of us singing together, and when he heard the result – the special, tight blend that we had straight away – he announced gleefully, 'My sugar babies!'

And so we that's how we began. We started out as the Sugar Babies but soon found out that the name had already been taken by an American gospel group, so had to change it. Cue: Sugababes.

Like me, the other girls seemed very comfortable in a studio environment; it was something that came naturally to all of us and felt a bit like fate. I was happy to spend hours at a time recording demos every day, which is what we did. The plan was that we'd record enough strong tracks to eventually secure a record deal with a major label. It was hard work, but I loved being in the studio – the whole vibe appealed to me.

Of course, away from parents and teachers I was eating loads of rubbish fast food – Chinese takeaways or food from Kebab Kids, or Tootsies restaurant round the corner, which had the best waffles and ice cream – and I started putting on a bit of weight. I'd sing, eat, sit, repeat over long days and even longer nights. I was also smoking cigarettes with Siobhan on the staircases, and got quite nifty at stealing other people's spliffs and sneaking out the back to puff on them whenever I could. It was

1998, and I was thirteen years old, living a life other teenagers could only dream of.

We probably worked many more hours at a time than you would do today, but it was all worth it. In my mind, I'd started on this road from a young age, singing for the Filipino community and performing in competitions all over Europe. This was what I was meant to do, and I was, and still am, eternally grateful to my dad for setting me on that path.

Looking back on those early days now, I wouldn't change a thing. I'd do it all again, though I'm not sure I'd have been happy with my own daughter working like that at thirteen. We really did work our arses off!

After Keisha had joined the band, I felt a lot more confident about blending my voice with others', perhaps because we'd sung together so many times in the past. Our producers would direct us, but we quickly learned who sounded best on each part and what our individual strengths were. Working with Don-E was fantastic and always a great learning experience. Because he was a vocalist, he really understood what he was asking us to do, and could help us with arranging harmonies and finding where we sat in the blend. I was blessed with a decent range – I could go high or low – and if there was a more airy vocal needed, I was your girl. There were other things that Siobhan and Keisha suited much more. Siobhan has a great mid/higher range and doesn't go too low. Keisha can go low but isn't particularly comfortable down there. Her voice sits beautifully between my voice and Siobhan's and is very strong and soulful. For us, those varying vocal styles became apparent quite quickly, so as far as who sang what goes, it depended on the song we were doing at the time. I love the fact that we have such individual styles. We could have all been clones and sounded the same, and that probably would have worked, but our blend wouldn't have been so distinctive and special as it was and has been ever since.

Usually, we all sang the parts that suited us best, but these days, I'll often try to avoid being the one opening the song; I tend to like singing the middle eight or the second verse. It's in my nature to want to sit back a little bit sometimes, but if the girls think I should sing the opening, they'll tell me.

'Mutya, can you just try it?'

'No, I don't want to do it.'

'Please, just try. You'll sound good on it.'

I always give in eventually because I know it's all about what's best for the track.

What's funny is that on some tracks, people often can't tell us apart anyway, despite our differences. Sometimes, we can't even tell one another apart! We'll be listening back and squabbling over who is who. I'll say, 'That's you, Keisha,' and she'll argue, 'No, Mutya, that's you!'

'Me?'

'Yes, and that bit is Siobhan.'

'Is it? I thought it was you!'

It's interesting now, listening back to those early recordings – some of which I only have on cassette tape – because I feel like our distinct sound was established very early on. We sound the same today as we did back then, although there was a bit more of a chipmunk quality to some of it when we were young. It was all super-cute and very high, but that strong familiar blend was very much there right from the start.

That's not to say that later versions of the line-up weren't great too; they were just different, perhaps more polished.

But what really hit about the Mutya-Keisha-Siobhan blend was its rawness. We sang until we got it right, and what we recorded was what you heard, no messing. Nowadays, when we're recording, one of us will do something a bit off, and the producer will say, 'Oh, don't worry, I can edit it later.' Attitudes like that can be quite frustrating. We go into the studio as professionals, wanting to perfect the vocals ourselves, without technology. But I think sometimes producers feel that because they have that technology at their fingertips, they might as well use it, to save time more than anything.

These days, people can make records in their bedroom on a laptop, which is amazing, but also means that part of the craft of producing records seems to have been lost. I used to love watching the producers and engineers committing things to tape and editing parts by literally cutting tapes with a blade and splicing them together. Before digital took over, we could watch the tapes rewinding on a 24-track machine, back to the parts we needed to re-sing. And you did have to re-sing, much more so than now. These days, you can sing a bum note that can be fixed with a few clicks of a mouse, but at the time there was no such thing as Auto-Tune or Melodyne to make the vocals perfect. You just had to grind until you got it right. We worked hard at our craft and there was something cool about our slight imperfections; they're what helped give us that distinct Sugababes sound.

FOUR

LONDON RECORDS CAME IN RIGHT at ground level. Ron Tom already had a strong working relationship with them, having formed and managed All Saints, who'd had such success with the label before us. All I remember is having what felt like a million meetings with various departments, lawyers and record-company execs. It's all a bit of a blur to me now, how the music machine worked and how it all happened, but I do remember the day we signed our deal. My whole family were overjoyed, and it felt so exciting. It seemed unimaginable that I was about to start putting music out into the world, not to mention being handed a cheque for the kind of money I'd never even dreamed of.

In those days, advances, the money you got upfront when you were signed, were larger and easier to come by if you got a record deal. I was lucky enough to be able to buy a house for my parents with my advance, which made me very happy because I wanted to give something back to them.

Looking back, I feel like although the label believed in us, some people on the team felt like it was a risk, pushing such young girls out there and expecting a return. I guess it's not surprising. We were schoolgirls, and they were planning on putting big money behind us. I don't think that happens with a lot of artists now, and I have no idea how people survive while trying to make music and develop careers. These days, companies seem to be more interested in how many followers an artist has on social media. If you're not right up there with your numbers, they aren't interested. When I think about my Instagram followers, I'm pretty sure labels wouldn't be taking me seriously as a new artist. If Sugababes were going out there now, I don't think a major label would spit on us if we were on fire.

Luckily for us, things were different then, and there we were, signed to London Records, a major label – aged thirteen!

With a record deal in place, we had the recording of our first album ahead of us, plus rehearsals and a certain amount of media training – probably not enough in hindsight. We were just three teenagers from north-west London, and none of us had a clue how to present ourselves or behave when it came to the interviews and appearances that would come with any success. I definitely needed help in that department, and I'm not sure I had enough in those early days. In an odd way, I think our unpolished nature ended up being part of our appeal. We came across as authentic. It still makes me cringe, though. When I look back on some of my first interviews, I'm giving 'not bothered' and 'can't be arsed to be here'. In my early interviews, I could barely manage to mumble an answer. When I see them now, I think, *My god, Mutya, do something, say something, what's wrong with you?*

The truth was, I wasn't really prepared for the publicity side of things, at least not to any great extent. I was a teenager who would rather be singing in the studio or hanging out with her friends than doing interviews. Nobody told me I had to smile; in fact, I think the people running our careers liked the idea that I had an attitude. It suited the direction that the Sugababes' image was headed – natural, unfussy, edgy. Siobhan and Keisha were much better at interviews than me, so

I just fell into the role of being the Babe with the attitude, and that continued for a while.

For our first record, we worked with various songwriters and producers: as well as Don-E, we worked with Jonny Rockstar, Cameron McVey and writer Felix Howard, who we still work with now. Felix has been in the industry for years. He's now the director of A&R at BMG but was famous as a child for being photographed by Jamie Morgan for the cover of *The Face* magazine and also for co-starring with Madonna in the video for her single 'Open Your Heart' in 1986. He's a legend. Cameron and Felix were part of the team who wrote what would be our first single, 'Overload', in 2000.

Most of our early recordings took place at Matrix Studios in Fulham, which was once part of an old church. That place was virtually a second home to us. You'd find us there most afternoons and evenings, singing our hearts out, or writing, or meeting new producers. We worked long hours over those two years. That's how long it took from becoming a band to release. It was our first record, so it had to be right. We were young and had time on our side, so nobody wanted to rush out something for the sake of it.

There were days when we'd go straight from school to the studio, rocking up in our school uniforms, and wouldn't leave again until six or seven a.m after working through the night. The studio was all the way over in Fulham – quite a trek back to north-west London – which often meant going home, getting washed and changed and going right back out to school again.

Luckily, I had plenty of energy, and there was plenty of food. There were also always loads of people milling in and out of the studio, who we met and mingled with. They brought fresh energy with them. I enjoyed that side of it, but more and more

I started to miss my non-industry friends and my family too. There were times when I had to miss out on birthdays and other special occasions, which, being the family-orientated person I am, was upsetting. Whenever that happened, I would keep telling myself that it would all be worth it. At least I had Keisha and Siobhan to share the journey with. We were close and we had a lot in common. It would have been much harder doing it alone.

The other downside of all this was that I didn't get to see school through to the end. As things got busier and busier with late-night studio sessions and days away, I had to make the decision to leave – we all did. It was just too difficult to schedule all the Sugababes' stuff with regular school days, so it was one or the other and the music always won out. There were weeks when we'd only make it into school for one or two days, and once you miss that much you have no chance of catching up. It's strange to think that I was only in Year 9 at that point. We didn't completely give up on our education; we had tutoring from then on, right through to our GCSEs. The tutors would come to the studio to teach us when we had downtime, but it wasn't the same as being in a classroom with all your mates, getting into trouble and causing mayhem.

I missed the school environment and, looking back, I wish I hadn't left. For the short time I was there, I had a great group of friends. I don't like the word 'popular' when it comes to kids, but I felt that I was well liked. I wish there'd been a way I could have been in the band but carried on with proper schooling. It just seemed impossible at the time.

There came a point, down the line, when Keisha and I asked if we could go back, but the school wouldn't take us. Once we were gone, we were gone. There had been a certain amount of resentment about us leaving to pursue a music career, and most

people thought we'd never make anything of it. Even some of
the people I'd thought were my friends were cold towards me
once I'd left. Some of my school mates didn't want to hang out
or even talk to me any more, which really upset me. I felt dis-
owned and let down, all because I was trying to step outside of
the norm and do something different.

Leaving school at such a young age also meant missing out
on what might have come after. I'd love to have had the experience of art college or university – not just the education but
the social aspect too. As a band, we were always surrounded
by people who were older than us, which is probably why, in
the early days, I was always so eager to rush back to my mates
on the estate. It was amazing to see all of these creative people
at work, but there wasn't any room for just being a kid. Even
as I got a bit older, those girly trips and holidays some of my
friends were going on weren't available to me. I was a very late
starter when it came to all that.

I sometimes wonder how my life might have turned out and
what kind of person I'd be if I had gone down the road of education. Maybe I'd have been a renowned artist, or maybe I'd be
married with five kids – or both!

In the end, I can't complain; my life has been blessed in
so many other ways because of the choices I made, and I've
had some great life experiences. But yes, there will always be
regrets. For me it never felt like just a job; it was a way of life.

One of the few places we were actually able to let loose and
just be teenagers was the under-18s garage scene. Siobhan was
the one who first introduced me to those nights. We'd often go
together, dressed up to the nines, and Keisha came a few times
too. The look back then for girls was short black skirts with a

mini-split at the side, or pedal pushers and loafers, paired with tiny crop-tops or coloured satin shirts, and PVC hairbands. Whatever we were wearing, we'd soon get hot and sweaty dancing our arses off. I would lose myself in the music; I loved what they were playing. It was nights like these that really kept my passion for music alive. I loved how the DJs mixed and blended the music, dictating the mood of the room. A lot of the DJs at those nights went on to become successful garage MCs, and I'm still friends with some of them today.

Although these were under-18 events, we could always get our hands on alcohol if we wanted to. There were people slipping in with Hooch and Smirnoff Ice, plus we could always have a sneaky drink before going in.

Of course, there were lots of boys there too. Since we'd left school, this was the only chance we had to be around boys our age, and I definitely didn't let that opportunity go to waste! I don't know what my parents would have thought, seeing me sandwiched in between two guys, grinding against me on the dancefloor, but I was always the girl in the middle and right in the thick of it. In fact, it was at one of those raves that I had my first kiss – at Sine Bar in Rayners Lane with a boy called Tyrone. He was lovely – six foot tall with big, juicy lips.

On these nights out, I'd often stay at Siobhan's house. I loved going round; there was always such a nice vibe and her parents were more lenient than mine. I wasn't usually allowed to stay over at friends' houses or even to stay away from home for school stuff, but with Siobhan it was different. I think it was because my parents knew her parents and we were working together professionally. Our friendship just seemed that little bit more grown up. Siobhan also had a good friend who was Filipino, who happened to be my brother Kris's girlfriend. All

of that made Dad feel more relaxed, so he let me stay over with
Siobhan regularly.

One of the key things I remember about being at her house
was the shampoo. Siobhan's family always had decent products
in her bathroom, including Aussie shampoo and conditioner.
I fell in love with the smell of the shampoo and used it at every
opportunity. To this day it always reminds me of her.

Even though my dad was quite chilled about me going to
the under-18s raves, the deal was that my brother always had
to come and pick me up. He'd wait for me outside, and I had
to make sure to meet him on time or Dad would lose his shit.

The raves were a regular thing, all through the period when we
were recording our album up until our first release, which took
a while. We'd got together in a band in 1998, but didn't release
anything until September 2000 – our debut single, 'Overload'.
By then, we'd recorded our entire album, *One Touch*, already.
That's how the process worked back in the day. You'd sign an
album deal, and record the whole thing before you released
anything. It's very different now. Often artists will come up
with a good track and just put it out, whether or not there's an
album or campaign ready. The methods of releasing music are
so much more accessible now, with streaming platforms. You
don't have to wait and plan for the creation of physical products.

The video for 'Overload' was, I think, very classy and naturally cool. Directed by Phil Poynter, it's shot against a white
background, a camera tracking across the three of us singing in various outfits. It's quite simple and very 'fashion'!
We all look serious through most of it, so the candid shots
of Keisha and me laughing that come towards the end bring
something sweet.

The strangest thing about being on that first video shoot was having so many people running around after us. There was always someone on hand asking if we wanted drinks, if we were hungry, asking what we might want for dinner. There were wardrobe people steaming our clothes, stylists dressing us, and a glam-squad retouching our hair and make-up every five minutes. When you've always done everything yourself, that environment feels odd, and I found it hard to get used to all the 'How can I help you?' people surrounding us. It felt like they were treating us as if we were stars already, but at the time it was hard to think of myself in that way. I was over-whelmed by it, but it being our first video I also felt pressure to keep them all happy. Everyone seemed to have their own vision of how we should be and what we should look like, and I went along with it because I was too shy to say, 'No, I don't like that.' I guess I was just eager to please.

My look was very different back then, quite effortless. There were no stick-on lashes or hair extensions – it was all just me. There was a cuteness and vulnerability in all of our looks, and I appreciate how natural we all were. I was always anti-fake anything. I didn't even want to wear make-up in those days. As time went on, having my make-up and styling done quickly became my least favourite part of doing videos and photo shoots. I couldn't stand people touching my face and telling me what to wear. I put up with it for a while, but as we got busier and every day had a tight, packed schedule, there was always a hairdresser, a stylist or a make-up artist touching or prodding me, and I hated it. I started to push back and complain if it got too much.

The best thing about filming that first day was how comfortable I felt in front of the camera. I'd had such a lot of experience of performing by then, I just saw it as an extension of that. That side of the video shoot, the actual performance, felt easy and enjoyable.

Before the release of the single, there was a fair bit of anticipation and nervousness on all our parts. As great as I thought the song was, I worried that people wouldn't like it and that it would be a flop. Suddenly, the moment had come where the label were hoping to see a return on their investment. What if we tanked? That's always been my go-to, imagining the worst-case scenario. To this day, I always step out on stage convinced that I'm going to be staring at an empty room and that there'll be nobody in the audience.

I needn't have worried. When 'Overload' came out in September 2000 it flew into the top ten. It went to number six on its first week of release, and was critically acclaimed, not only in the pop press but in national papers too. Digital Spy said it was one of the best debut singles by a British girl group.

It was when I heard we were going to be appearing on *Top of the Pops* that I knew things were going the right way. I was buzzing. It was one of those landmark TV shows that everyone watched back in the day. Growing up, I'd come home from school on a Friday, where Mum would have good old fish fingers, chips and baked beans on the table, and we'd all settle down and watch *Top of the Pops*. And then it would be all anyone talked about on Monday morning. As far as I was concerned, the fact that I was now going to be appearing on that iconic music show myself, as a performer, meant that I'd truly made it.

On the day of the recording, I remember feeling so scared while I was getting ready. Aside from the importance of the show itself, this was live singing in front of a living, breathing studio audience who were within touching distance. Not to mention that the show was beaming into the homes of millions of people. It was also the first time most of those people were going to see as well as hear us. This first impression really counted. Basically, it wasn't the sort of thing you wanted to fuck up!

The recording was all over in a flash. We did the song a couple of times to get different camera angles, but it all happened so quickly, there wasn't even time to think. I re-watched it the other day, and it was obvious we were all very nervous, sitting there on our stools, looking all aloof and full of attitude. The truth was, we didn't really know what we were doing or how to be.

That perceived air of moodiness became our trademark, the thing that set us apart from the more smiley, perfect girl bands who were around at that time. It wasn't something we tried to do; it was more a case of our youth, inexperience and slight shyness shining through.

Consequently, Sugababes became known as the cool, moody group with a *don't give a fuck* attitude. Young people saw it as fresh and real, and they got on board with it. That vibe made everyone think we were much older than we were at first. People couldn't believe it when they found out I was so young – that I was on TV with a top ten single at the age of fifteen. Neither could I!

Top of the Pops was such an important part of being an artist in those days. Once we'd done it, we'd made our mark and people knew who we were. After that night, our lives changed for ever. This happened pretty much immediately when we started making public appearances. We were suddenly hearing fans and the paparazzi calling out our names to get our attention. It was jarring at first. *God, these people know me now. They know my name!* It was a weird feeling and took some getting used to. While we were working on the album, we were still unknown to the world. We could still go to the shops without being recognized. Though our daily lives were totally different from the average school girl, to the public we still looked like kids. Then, after our first TV appearances, we weren't just ordinary girls any more. People looked at us differently.

There were a lot more TV music shows back then. Apart from *Top of the Pops*, there was *SMTV* and *CD:UK* on ITV, to name a few. When we did these shows, we would get to meet our growing crowd of fans, and I started to recognize a load of them who would turn up and wait outside the TV studios every time we appeared. It was very exciting suddenly having fans and knowing that people were into our music – and not just the kids who were into pop. We managed to achieve the cool vibes of some of the indie bands, so somehow appealed to the *NME* crowd too. We even got invited to the NME Awards ceremonies, which was rare for a pop group. *NME* even sponsored our first tour. That was what was great about Sugababes: we couldn't be pigeonholed. We could do the Smash Hits Poll Winners' Party, the Brits, the MOBOs and the NME Awards, because we had that wide cross-genre appeal.

I particularly loved being on MTV. It was such a huge thing at the time, and we often got to mix with the other pop stars and bands of the day. These were the pinch-me moments when I'd be in a room with super-famous people thinking, *I'm actually fucking here.* I also loved the dress-up of it all, the fun and party atmosphere of it, a new outfit and hairstyle for every appearance. I could be a different person every day if I wanted to. I really felt like a star. I still cherish the memory of all that, because, to a certain extent, that heyday of pop glamour seems to have disappeared.

The more shows we did, the bigger these crowds became. We could see our fame growing in real time. I'd see these girls hanging around and think, *Oh, it's you again . . . and you.* These young kids were leaving their houses at stupid o'clock in the morning to come see us for a few hot seconds every week. It was a good feeling knowing we had fans who were so keen to follow us, so dedicated, but I couldn't help worrying, some of them being so young. *Where do they get their money from?* I wondered. Some of them even had their parents dropping them off just to hang around outside the studio. They were dedicated, and there are a few of them who still come to our shows and performances now. I'm always happy to see them.

Back then, there were times when we didn't even have a moment to stop and say hello because our schedules were so tight, and I always felt guilty that we had to run. At moments like that I almost envied the fans sometimes, wishing I could be the one hanging out with my friends with nothing much to do, obsessing over a group we loved. In reality, of course, I wouldn't have traded places for the world. I knew I was lucky to be where I was, and getting to sing for a living was a dream come true, but the thoughts were there. Our fans were a constant reminder of the youth we'd given up. Seeing them waiting outside studios for us in all weathers was another sign that my life had changed and would never be the same again. In one way or another, I was always being watched, if not by our fans, then by our management, a camera lens or by the media and paparazzi. We were growing up in front of people's faces and in front of the camera. I don't have to try to remember how I looked and acted as a kid because I only have to google myself to look at the teenage me. It's all there. Someone is always watching, even now. It's been like that since I was fourteen.

I struggled with it in those early days, and for a long time after. I have suffered from depression and anxiety over the years, and to this day, I have to control where my mind goes and how I think. My dad always says I'm a loose cannon and that when I explode, it's hard to bring me back down. I have more of a handle on it today; less so when I was younger.

My escape back then was to go out and enjoy myself, but I didn't always make the best choices. Instead of pacing myself, I went all out, chasing as much fun as I could find, trying to make up for the youth I was missing out on. Of course, when you're famous you're suddenly on the guest list everywhere you go.

In the world I found myself in, life moved quickly, and many things were accessible to us – opportunities, good and bad.

We also met a lot of people, most of them older but not always wiser. Some of the adults we dealt with cared more about our worth than our well-being. As long as we were making money for them, they couldn't give two shits about what was going on in our heads or our hearts as children. Making money was important to us too, as a band, and we really felt that pressure. True, record deals were more lucrative in those days, but if you got signed for half a million, you were expected to pay that money back through record sales. We had to recoup our advance, so the work couldn't stop. Even now, that hasn't really changed. I have bills to pay and I can't just stop if and when I feel like it.

When I was younger, it would have been helpful to me if somebody had stopped me and said, 'Let's not worry about money, let's make sure this girl is OK.' But that just wasn't the culture at the time.

Thank God for my family during that period; they were the ones I could always rely on. But even they weren't strong enough to stop what was to come.

FIVE

'OVERLOAD' WAS A BIG HIT, not just in the UK but throughout Europe, Australia and New Zealand, and so all of a sudden
we were travelling to all sorts of places doing TV and radio
promos. Though I never really saw much of the places we visited. Moving through at 100 miles per hour – airports, cars,
hotels and venues – there was never time to stop and appreciate.

We were very popular in Germany, so there were a lot of
trips there, splitting our time between Munich and Frankfurt.
I have so many memories of being in Germany, and one year,
hardly coming back to the UK at all.

During the early days of Sugababes, I had my family around
me a fair bit. My mum had her chaperone licence from when I
used to tour with Pipa, so was an obvious choice to travel with
us, and my dad often drove us around to various appearances
and gigs.

As close as I was to my parents, though, it was sometimes
hard knowing they were always there and watching my every
move. When it was announced that we would be doing a
promo in Australia, I was relieved to find out that neither
Mum nor Dad would be joining us. As much as I loved them,
it felt like they were cramping my style. What teenager wants
their parents around when they're hanging with their friends?

It was quite freeing having a neutral, much younger chaperone tagging along instead.

With regular trips, we met so many new people – our world opened up. The fact that people knew who we were in all these different countries felt surreal. I'd often meet fans and walk away wondering how they knew so much about me. It's not like there was social media back then; this was all through our records, videos, TV appearances and, of course, *Top of the Pops* and magazines like *Smash Hits*.

With no Google or Instagram, fans had to go out and spend money to find out about us – and they did! It was wild to imagine that people were saving up their cash to spend on me! And not just on the mags but on our CDs too. Before streaming, you really had to invest in music you liked. I spent many hours in HMV, listening to each album on headphones, carefully skipping through the tracks to decide whether or not to buy it.

Fans hung around everywhere we went – boys and girls alike. They were always outside the hotel, and it fascinated me, that idea of standing outside a building, just hoping to get a glimpse of someone. It's wasn't that I didn't want our fans around – as I said, I sometimes envied them – it just wasn't something I imagined doing myself. Maybe it's because I was in the public eye at such a young age and didn't have the time! It was even more weird to think that it was me they were trying to get a look at. Surely they knew I was just an ordinary kid like them? Wasn't I?

As cool as it was having eager fans and admirers, most of whom were lovely, there were the odd few that took things a step too far. One night, while I was alone in my hotel room, somebody knocked on the door. It was late, so I peeked through the little peephole in the door and saw a guy standing there with flowers. I couldn't really see what he looked like, only that I didn't have a clue who he was. I was suddenly shit-scared. We always used fake names whenever we checked into hotels, so I couldn't work out how this dude had found my room unless he'd followed me from somewhere else. His intentions could have been harmless, but the idea that someone would have gone to the trouble of doing all that was unsettling, especially seeing how young I was, and so far from home. I guess this experience made me realize just how much had changed in my life. As much as I was still trying to be that happy, ordinary girl, things were very different now. I'd tried to ignore it, but I couldn't any more.

Of course, I never did open the door to Flower Boy, and eventually he left, but for the next few nights I had to sleep in Keisha's room just in case he came back.

In the early days of our success, I was quite blasé about it. Having chart success or a top ten record didn't really register with me, at least not in the way it should have. What really mattered to me was knowing that our music was out there and people were enjoying it. Aside from that, I was genuinely more concerned with what fun I could have outside the band or whether I was missing a party. It was as if I was there but not there. I did my job and I worked hard, but I didn't really care what happened after that job was done. In truth, I had zero fucks to give! For me, the real fun was singing, performing and creating music. All the other stuff that came with it didn't light my fire.

As many great things as we had going on around us, I sometimes found being in a band full-time hard. It wasn't the kind of job you could just switch off from easily – it becomes your whole life. At the end of a working day, I was always the one itching to rush home so I could just hang out and mess around. I still had those childlike longings inside me. Often, I would come off stage after a show or an important appearance and leave without even saying goodbye. Before anyone even knew I was gone, I'd be in the car, texting or calling my mates to let them know I was on my way back. I didn't like to feel I was being left out. Even when I was out there travelling the world and doing the sorts of things most teenagers would give anything to do, I couldn't shake the feeling that something was missing. My happy place was still hanging out with my friends around the estate.

I sometimes wonder what I must have looked like to others back then: some ungrateful, fucked-up teenager who just wanted to get 'mash-up' with her friends instead of appreciating the amazing opportunities she'd been given? I enjoyed my work and all the travel and excitement that came with being in Sugababes. And of course, I loved getting to work with the girls every day. But teenagers just have different priorities! I'm sure it must have been hard for the other girls in the group, me being the way I was. I always had one foot out of the door, but at the time I was so wrapped up in what I wanted to do, I just couldn't see it.

It sometimes makes me smile, thinking of myself then, rolling my eyes and complaining because I had to go do *Top of the Pops*. All I could think about was getting back to my mates on the estate – and we were proper little tearaways too. When I was back with them, it felt like nothing had changed. I was back to my old mischief. Some days, Mum would give me a note to take to the corner shop giving me permission to buy cigarettes for her. '*Please can you sell my daughter a pack of cigarettes with my permission.'* Of course, you know I kept those notes to use again when me and my friends fancied a ciggie. Back home, away from the cameras and the industry officials, I could be a classic rebellious teen, smoking weed in the alleyways, or drinking Hooch or Smirnoff Ice when we could get our hands on it. Sometimes the police would chase us down alleyways, so we'd jump over the walls of the local synagogue to hide from them.

As time passed and I got older, I started to venture further outside the estate.

'Mum, I'm going up to the top of the hill,' I'd shout, running out of the front door.

Up there, I'd talk and chill with a couple of other girls I knew from the area, Dawn and Danielle, who I still chat with every so often. The three of us were always getting up to no good. Despite all of the huge success I was experiencing, I wanted to keep doing all those fun things. I was still a young kid, trying to get away with the same stuff my mates were getting away with.

I was so desperate to be just like everyone else that I hadn't quite clocked that my newfound fame meant I was more conspicuous than I used to be. Some situations I got myself into around that time were downright dangerous, and when I look back now it makes my blood go cold to think of what could have happened if I hadn't had my wits about me.

One afternoon, I bunked off my tutoring session to meet up with an older guy I'd been introduced to by one of my friends. I told some of my other mates at school what I was doing, and to make sure they answered their phones if I called because I didn't really know the guy I was meeting. Stupidly, I got into the guy's car as soon as we met and the next thing I knew, he was driving me to his flat in north London whether

I liked it or not. It all felt OK at first because he was polite and acting fairly normal, but the fact that I didn't know exactly where I was going made me nervous. At one point, as we neared his place, we passed a bus garage I recognized and I made a mental note of exactly where I was, just in case.

Once I stepped out of the car and into his tiny ground-floor studio flat, his mood changed quickly. Inside, he locked the door and then threw the key out of the window, knowing I could see what he was doing. I couldn't believe my eyes. If this guy was trying to scare me, he was doing a fucking great job, because I had no clue what to do next. All I could think was, *Fuck, this guy has kidnapped me.*

Rather than kicking off and making a scene, I sat nervously next to him as we watched TV in the dark for a while, but the atmosphere was charged, and he seemed on edge. Then, without warning, he launched himself on me, and when I tried to pull away, he started dragging me by my jeans towards the bedroom. By then, I knew what was about to happen. I felt my jeans ripping and tearing, my legs exposed, but he didn't stop pulling at me, dragging me towards his bed, with me yelling and cursing at him. As he pushed me down and climbed on top of me, I yelled and fought, kicking my feet like crazy while he did his best to keep me pinned down. All I could see was this determined face looking down on me like I had no choice in what was going down. When I found my arms momentarily free, I slapped him and shoved him off me, then jumped up and headed for the kitchen area. Spotting an open window, I pulled myself upward and climbed out. Breathing hard on the pavement, I thanked God we were on the ground floor and that he hadn't come after me. By now it was dark outside, and I couldn't be sure this guy wouldn't change his mind and try his luck again. Shaking, I pulled out my phone and called one of the friends I'd put on standby, who, by some miracle, was at the bus garage I'd passed on the way, just across the road from where I was now standing. I looked over, saw his car and ran towards it. At that moment, I felt like my friend might be saving me from something terrible; the relief I felt, jumping into his car, was unbelievable.

I never made a complaint or reported the guy who attacked me, because that would mean admitting my own stupidity to my family and friends. I didn't even tell my brothers, because they were crazy boys at the time and I knew what they'd have done. Still, I never went near the guy or spoke to him again. He lived in an area relatively close to me, so I was always worried I might bump into him, but as much as I could, I pushed him and the incident out of my mind. A long time afterwards, I found out he'd died of cancer and I didn't know how to feel about it. I'd always doubted that I was the first girl he'd done that to, and I probably wasn't the last.

I know what would've happened if I hadn't fought him off that day, what the outcome would have been, and it made me angry. Both at him, and at myself for being in that position in the first place. If I could talk now to the younger Mutya, I would slap her round the face and say, 'You could have done better. You *should* have done better!' Thank God, that day I had told a handful of friends what I was doing and one of them was there when I needed him.

This experience had, in some ways, come out of me being reckless and naive. Back then I thought nothing bad could ever happen to me.

Despite being in the public eye, I never thought of myself as famous or set myself above anyone else, and my behaviour reflected that. Some of my close friends warned me to take care, reminding me that I wasn't ordinary or invisible any more and that certain people would automatically view me differently because of who I was, whether I liked it or not. They were right. While for the most part it was a positive thing, not thinking I was better than anyone else and treating others how I'd want people to treat me, there were some who were bound to take advantage of that. I always wanted to be out in the world and doing things, getting up to all sorts like other kids my age, but this experience made me realize that I didn't have that safety any longer. While I strived to see the best in most people, sometimes there were other agendas at play and people would target me because of who I was.

There were many good things that happened to me as a teenager, some that other girls my age could only imagine. I was in the Babes, experiencing the joys of being a recording artist and performer, and there was so much to look forward to. The thing I was yet to learn was how to balance fame with everyday life. If I was going to stay safe, I had to accept that I wasn't just a regular teenager, and couldn't always do the things a normal teenager did. Still, that didn't stop me from trying. I clung on to my other life, hanging out with my friends, being at home with my loved ones. To me, one was never more important than the other. I think that's what kept me grounded – at least it did for a while.

SIX

OUR ALBUM *ONE TOUCH* CAME out in November 2000, one month after we'd had such huge success with 'Overload'. It peaked at number 26 on the album chart, which wasn't the smash I'd hoped for. I was disappointed with that, but because the album went gold and reached the top ten in Germany, Switzerland and Austria we knew we still had something worth pursuing. Our success in Europe also meant more travel to those places for promotion. We were out promoting more than ever, and during all that madness we were all busy studying for our GCSEs. Siobhan's school eventually allowed her to go back, but Keisha and I had to continue with tutors.

I still have one of our old schedules from that time. There was one year when we had just one day off. It was an extremely intense lifestyle, especially given this was all before I had even turned sixteen. Studios, interviews, flights, TV appearances: when the schedule is so tightly packed, you don't have time to think or just be. There were times when we were on four flights in a day, always with our chaperones in tow and sometimes the tutor as well. Not that there would have been time to sit down and take a class anyway. Learning was always secondary to performing, and that did cause difficulties for me, especially during my exams. I didn't feel like I was ready or that I'd done enough, so I just had to try my hardest and do the best I could.

My experiences with tutoring were mixed. Our teachers were always changing and we never knew quite what we were going to get with each new situation. We covered a lot of subjects: maths, English, science, art – everything that we needed to give us a full education and get us through our upcoming exams. At first, we had tutors come to the recording studio in Fulham. I felt bad for some of them. Most of the time after a long session in the studio, we struggled to concentrate on schoolwork. At that point in the day, we just wanted to blow off steam, and it was a tough task to try to stop us messing around. One of the tutors had a few whisps of hair that he swept across his head in a bad comb-over. When he sat opposite us, glaring down at a book in concentration, Keisha and I would gently blow on his hair, so it lifted off his head and flipped the other way. His head would come up sharply, and we'd be sitting there looking innocent while he looked around as if to say, *Where the hell is that breeze coming from?* Poor guy. He must've hated us.

Not long after that, we started going to see an Italian lady, for the sake of the story let's call her Alessia, who lived in a big, beautiful house in Kilburn. The house was set up with different living spaces on different floors. Her oldest son lived on the top floor, and the floor below had a few more bedrooms and a bathroom. Her daughter lived on the ground floor, but I was never sure where Alessia's room was because the house was so massive.

By then, Siobhan had gone back to high school to do her exams, and Keisha didn't stay with Alessia long either. For me, her place was convenient because a lot of my friends lived nearby so I could easily slip off and meet them if the mood took me. On some days, I'd get picked up by a driver, arrive at the house, stay a little while in the morning and then go missing for the entire rest of the day. As far as tutors went, Alessia was a good one but quite lenient, at least she was with me. She never seemed to mind that I'd go missing for hours. In fact, sometimes she'd even call me when I was AWOL and ask if everything was OK, never demanding that I come straight back to class, which is where I should have been.

One of the great things about Alessia's place was that her fridge was always full of goodies. In fact, at one point, she gave me a whole fridge there, stocked full of food that she'd bought especially for me. Alessia was very good in that way, she would cook meals for me, and every morning had one of those sweet sachet coffees ready for my arrival. Sometimes, I even stayed at the house overnight, and she'd let me invite friends over – yes, even boys!

It was at Alessia's house where I lost my virginity, aged sixteen. Up until then, I hadn't had much experience with boys. I was a typical teenage girl, talking to several different guys at any one time without getting too serious. I was very shy when it came to the opposite sex. In fact, I'd sometimes get Keisha to talk to boys that I liked because I didn't have the bottle. I didn't know what to say. I was bubbly and outgoing with girls, but with guys I wasn't that person. I was closed off and introverted. It's not surprising, having grown up with four older brothers who were always warning me against having boyfriends. In fact, for a long time they specifically told me I *couldn't have* a boyfriend. I remember once asking my older brother permission to go out with a boy who was interested in me, and he said, 'No.' So, I went back to the guy and said, 'I'm sorry, my brother told me I can't go out with you.' And that was the end of that. After a few years of this, it's no wonder I was rubbish at talking to guys!

The boy I lost my virginity to was someone I'd been friends with for some time. Before I'd left high school, I'd sometimes bunk off lessons and walk over to his school to meet some of my girlfriends who also went there. Theirs was a Catholic school, so I'd sneak into the chapel and hide out until my friends finished their class. Then at lunchtimes, or after school, we'd all hang at a nearby cafe that had a pool table. That was where I met Freddie, and we got close; I guess you could say he was my first boyfriend. Over time we started spending more and more time alone together until I mustered up the courage to invite him to Alessia's. There was no *way* I could bring him round to my house!

Alessia must have had an inkling about what was on the cards that day, because while I was chilling with Freddie in one of the bedrooms, she popped her head around the door and said, 'Make sure you wear protection,' before closing the door.

Freddie and I giggled nervously. We were both of consenting age, but neither of us were used to grown-ups speaking that way in our presence.

Looking back, I'm glad it happened that way. It was a safe environment for such a big thing to happen, and Freddie was a nice enough boy. It was never going to be a big romance, though, and eventually we went our separate ways.

In between all the fun and games, there was *some* learning going on. I was still in love with anything to do with art. Apart from making music, it was the thing I loved doing most, and my portfolio of paintings was bulging. As well as creating, I also studied art history, soaking up knowledge of the great painters and the classic periods. I put my whole heart into it and Alessia always encouraged me to pursue my interest. In fact, whenever I presented her with a new creation, she'd make me sign every single picture. After my GCSEs, the portfolio with all my beautiful work mysteriously disappeared. I was gutted, and we never found out what happened to it. My mum was convinced that Alessia had stolen it, knowing it might be worth something one day, now I was a pop star. I sometimes wonder if some of my original artworks will come up for sale on eBay one day!

SEVEN

AS AN OLDER SISTER, I should have probably tried to be a good influence on my younger siblings, but I was the opposite. As a kid, I loved body piercings, and I was always on at my dad to allow me to have them. I think I'd just turned twelve when I first asked him to take me to get my belly button pierced. By then, I'd already had my ears and nose pierced. When my sisters got to a similar age, I was already taking them to get piercings without checking with Mum and Dad if they were OK with it. My dad's reaction was always the same.

'Stop copying your sister!' he shouted at them.

There was little chance of them taking any notice of that. They loved the idea of piercings as much as I did, and it wasn't long before they both had their belly buttons pierced too.

Dad probably knew he was fighting a losing battle. By then, my family were all very aware that there was no taming my rebellious side. I had my own career now and was bringing in my own money, so it was harder to tell me what to do. Plus, the fact that I was so successful probably meant that I could get away with more. They were so proud of me. Mum and Dad were always my biggest supporters, right from the start. In fact, my entire family were one hundred per cent with me, and always have been. My mum still cries when she watches our shows. For my dad, I think my success was made even sweeter because he'd been the one who encouraged me to sing in the first place. He never stopped pushing me forward – even when I was leading my little sisters astray.

It wasn't just piercings either. I also took my sisters to their first nightclub. I don't know where my mind was, but one day I just thought, *Hey, wouldn't it be fun to take them clubbing!* I believed it would be a great experience for them, despite the fact that they were only about thirteen or fourteen years old. Looking back, I don't know how I got away with getting them inside. Part of it was knowing all the security people – the door staff and the bouncers – who didn't think to question me, and part of it was the fact that usually when I went out I was with a massive crowd of other people. The last thing door staff wanted was a ton of people lingering around on the street outside the club, so when I turned up with a big group, they'd get us inside as soon as possible. I guess my sisters just got swept through the door with everyone else.

As you've probably gathered by now, as a teenager, I loved going out to clubs and parties; I lived for it. In those days, in the early 2000s, London felt like the place to be. It was the city everyone was drawn to. There was positivity in the air and an essence of fun. Bars and clubs were open late, and they were thriving.

Before smartphones had amazing cameras, I took a little digital camera with me everywhere, and I have so many great pictures of groups of friends dancing and having the best time.

Nowadays, the rules against underage drinking and clubbing are mega-strict, but back then, IDs weren't even a thing. If you were on a guest list, you just went in. I can't even say my sisters looked older than their age, because they didn't. At the time, I didn't consider that I might be leading them down a bad path, and they certainly weren't heeding my dad's constant warnings either.

'Stop following your sister,' he would say over and over. 'Just stop!'

At the time, I just couldn't see where the harm was. My thought process then was, let them at least try all these things and then they can decide whether or not they like them and want to try them again.

That was the first night of many. I'd take my sisters and even some of their friends out to the trendiest clubs and even to some of the house raves and parties I went to. I was getting invited to so many big nights out during that period, and if I could get away with it, I would always take them with me. They enjoyed it as much as I did; we loved being out together. I was so often away with the Sugababes, so getting to do those things as sisters gave us a special closeness; a strong, unbreakable bond that still remains today.

Looking back now, taking them to an environment where there was alcohol and god knows what else was probably one of the more stupid things I did, and I wouldn't dream of exposing a young person to that now. I guess you live and learn.

The clubs in central London were amazing at the time – nightspots like Propaganda, CC Club, China White, the Embassy and so many others. These were all places I hung out at during my early Sugababes days, and I thrived there. For seven days a week, I had a full nightlife schedule. On a Monday, I'd be in Ten Rooms. They had a great live mic night, and all the American artists who were coming through town would end up performing there. Tuesdays would be Funky Buddha in Mayfair, Thursdays would be POP, and Friday would be Propaganda, where you'd walk in and see what seemed like half the music industry out partying, and then on to CC Club. I was very much the party girl, but being in the public eye and being so recognizable was a double-edged sword.

Getting into clubs for nothing and the free drinks that followed were, of course, a benefit, but the downside was having eyes on me the whole time. My main problem on these nights out was avoiding the press. I'd be enjoying myself and, yes, sometimes going a little crazy, but there were often consequences if there were reporters or paparazzi around, getting snap-happy. Can you imagine if the stupid things you did on nights out got put in the papers? Pre-social media and the internet explosion, everything was newspaper- and magazine-based, and it felt like certain areas of the media were more concerned with shame than truth. In those days, the paparazzi seemed to be hiding around every corner, and their MO was embarrassing their targets and trying to catch them in awkward situations.

At least there wasn't any camera-phone business back then. These days, with people sharing everything from their cat's breakfast to their wildest nights out, who knows what might have ended up on the internet. At least then, if someone was taking a picture, you generally knew about it.

I remember having a lot of 'can'ts' in my head – you can't do this, you can't do that. It was my own more reasonable inner voice trying to stop me from making a fool of myself, but I was never good at listening to that side of me. I tended to do whatever I wanted, and that's what sometimes landed me in the shit with the press. Several times, I had journalists or photographers deliberately try to upset me or cause an argument. They all knew how fiery I could be and that they'd always get a mouthful if they pissed me off.

Some mornings, I would go from the club straight to work. Sometimes, if I was just heading to the studio or a video shoot, I could get away with being hungover, or even still a bit tipsy from the night before, but live TV could be rough. When we performed on an early-morning show, like *GMTV* or *SMTV Live* with Ant and Dec on a Saturday, we'd sometimes get picked up as early as four a.m., depending on what time we were due on set. That was brutal. I'd only ever get an hour or two of sleep before I had to head in, and sometimes I didn't see my bed at all. It was just, in the door, get changed and head out again. Other partiers I can think of chose to wear dark glasses during those shows, but I hated wearing them. Instead, I'd carry a little bottle of brandy in my bag, or tequila, which I loved. Then, when no one was looking, I'd take a swig and it would perk me right up and help me get through the morning. If I hadn't done that, I'd have probably fallen asleep on live TV. I absolutely wouldn't recommend this to anyone now – it was all very wild-child – but you'd be surprised how often I was a little buzzed on daytime telly! At the time it felt like the necessary thing to do, but looking back, that was the start of my partying getting a little bit out of control.

By the early 2000s, people thought they knew me, and certain areas of the media judged me by what they saw on the outside. That cool persona our fans loved about us started being taken the wrong way by journalists. Some of the tabloid press called me moody and thought I had a bad attitude, simply because I didn't gush about everything during an interview. That just wasn't my style. I was keen to stay true to myself and not play up for the cameras. Although looking back at some of those interviews now makes me cringe, big time.

There was one with Cat Deeley on *CD:UK* where my apparent moodiness really shone through. The 'couldn't be arsed' attitude was even more obvious than usual, probably because I was perched on a couch next to Cheryl Tweedy and Victoria Beckham, who were sitting up and taking notice with relaxed, happy smiles, while I was slumped backwards with a face like fucking thunder. Watching it back recently, I was screaming at the TV – and my younger self – 'Sit up, Mutya! Crack a smile for god's sake!'

Cat was asking us about a selection of Christmas releases, and the possibility of Sugababes having a Christmas number one. This was a little further down the road, in 2003. We'd just released our single 'Too Lost In You' to coincide with the release of the film *Love Actually*, which featured the song on the soundtrack.

'If we'd had our choice, we would have released in January, we're not really bothered about it,' I said. 'I don't see the point of trying to have a big competition against everyone. A song's a song, so if it's gonna go to number one, it's gonna go to number one.'

I looked so miserable, but I just didn't realize how I was coming across at the time. I thought I was just being honest. What's more, it seemed to be a selling point for us as a band, that moodiness, especially when it came from me. At one point, *NME* invited me to do a piece where I was asked to either like a CD or smash it. They wanted the feistiness that I brought, so it was me they asked rather than the other girls. It felt like I was being told two different things. Some people loved that edge; others hated it.

It wasn't just my moodiness the press had a go at in those early days. They used to criticize everything from my body shape to my family, painting us as ghetto and somehow dodgy. They didn't look past what was on the outside to see the girl who loved her family, art, vintage clothes and old-school music. The girls call me 'Magic FM' because I'm always listening or singing along to all the old songs. If the tabloids had looked harder, they would have seen a girl who just loved going out and having fun with her friends. Sure, I loved a drink and a party, but if I'd been a footballer or some geezer from an indie band doing the same shit, no one would have batted an eyelid. There was so much about me that I would've loved the press to know, instead of the assumptions they were constantly printing.

It wasn't all bad. There were some magazines and publications, the cooler ones, more aimed at music fans and younger readers, who seemed to like the way I was. They got me and understood my attitude. I think they liked what they thought was the 'realness' of me – even though that might have been a little too real at times.

A lot of people who were listening to our music then were much older than we were. They were in their late teens or twenties while we were fifteen or sixteen at the start. I don't even think many fans knew just how young we were. With our edgier style came the assumption that we were older, and that affected how people would talk about us. They assumed we were adults, and doled out insults not knowing that we were just kids. Even out in public, when I got abused, the people handing it out were clearly unaware of my age. I'd have some older woman calling me a bitch in a club toilet and I'd say, 'Do you know this is a sixteen-year-old you're calling names? What's that about?'

Let's ignore the fact that I shouldn't have been there in the first place and that I didn't give a fuck anyway.

The newspapers on the other hand had the facts – so you'd think they would have known better than to pile criticism about someone's family or looks on to such young women.

Despite managing to keep some of the darker sides of my social life out of the press, I felt bullied by the media. There was nothing they let slide. I could do something as simple as placing my hand on my tummy, and someone would write that I was pregnant. Someone else would write that I was fat or miserable or a mess – the list went on. Looking back, I'm trying to imagine how anyone felt it was acceptable to do that to a teenager. Who were the people sitting at their desks that thought, *OK, today, I'm going to destroy a seventeen-year-old girl for the entertainment of the nation?*

I did not deserve to be insulted and torn down by people who didn't know me. The way the press talked about women, let alone teenagers, making assumptions about what they should or shouldn't be, was wrong, but it happened and it felt relentless.

My reaction to all this was to push back, to rebel even more. Nobody was going to tell *me* how to look or act. This only made the press jump on me even more. Their attitude was, *OK, you want to be yourself? That's fine, but we're going to attack you for it.*

It wasn't just salacious stories and insults either. The specific offence of 'upskirting' only became a crime in 2019. In the early 2000s, I regularly suffered paparazzi photographers taking pictures up my skirt, or trying to, when I was still under eighteen. I was always angry but had to control myself. I was smart enough to know that if I lashed out at them or fought them, I'd probably end up in court. They knew that too, which is why they got away with it. It wasn't just me either; it happened to many women in the public eye. Today, it wouldn't be allowed. Today, it would be them in court. But in those days there was nothing that could protect us from the leeches. We deserved better.

It was rare that I went out with Keisha or Siobhan back then, just because we all had different groups of friends. We each had our own vibe with our own social groups, and because we saw so much of one another during work hours or at industry events, it felt like we were always together anyway. I suppose that's why when I wasn't working I wanted my own space; time with my own friends who weren't necessarily attached to music or my day job. It's so different now, back working with Siobhan and Keisha once again. These days, I love being with them outside of work. I'm just so happy to be around them.

It's very much an age thing, and back then I guess my friends were the wilder crowd. None of them knew how to stay in their houses. They were a huge group, some of them I'd known since high school, and others who lived in the local area. On summer weekends when I wasn't working, we'd find a nice pub – one where we could sit outside and smoke – and we'd chill in the sun, drinking pints of cold beer. Oh yes, I love a pint! As well as the friends, there were the friends of friends, so the group would expand and grow. I suppose it wouldn't have been different to many groups of young people back then, but we were meeting every single day. Nobody in that group seemed to have a job at that time, apart from me, that is.

Having more money than most of them, I tried to share and be generous with others. Looking back, though, I was probably overgenerous and spent more than I should, sometimes to a ridiculous degree. There were times when I'd hear little digs and notice underhand guilt trips about what I was doing and what I had, and I didn't want to be seen as the person who didn't share her good fortune. I ended up overcompensating – as if I owed people something. I was young and, I suppose, a people-pleaser. Something I strive not to be these days.

It's no fun partying on your own, so I was always inviting people out and offering to pay if they couldn't afford it. I sometimes think, remembering the amount of cash I burned through back in the day, that if I'd stayed on my arse at home a bit more often I'd be a multi-millionaire by now. In the pre-Uber era, I had an Addison Lee taxi account, and the bill for that was off the charts. Instead of telling my mates to all meet me in one place, I was getting cars to pick up from this house, then another, then another. Because everyone was local, I didn't think it would be an issue, and I certainly didn't think about the bill I was racking up with cars waiting outside people's houses when they weren't even ready to leave. Oh god, the waiting-time charges! When we all got into our cars at the end of the night, there'd always be someone on the street talking while the meter ticked away. At one point, my bill was up to fifteen grand over a few months.

Eventually, as I got older, I realized that even if I went on my own, I'd see people I knew, so I didn't have to take a whole bunch of friends with me everywhere I went. I do look back and think, *What the fuck was I on, spending so much money just to keep other people sweet?*

People took advantage in other ways too. One boy I was dating around that time was lovely at first, but there was something slightly off about his behaviour. Often, after club nights, he'd head off with his brother and my friend in tow. I was still quite naive when it came to boys. I'd been so busy with work that I'd not had much time to make romantic mistakes, and at that point feeling jealous wasn't something that crossed my mind.

Down the line, not only did I find out my so-called boy-friend was sleeping with my friend, but that he also had a child I knew nothing about. Talk about clueless! I'd been in his car dozens of times and seen the baby seat, which he told me was for his niece or nephew, and never questioned it. As for my friend, she was very upfront and unapologetic about the sex.

'My pussy is my pussy,' she told me. She didn't give a shit.

As you can probably imagine, she's not one of the people I've remained close to.

I might've been devastated, but it turned out the guy really wasn't the right one for me anyway. I found out after we'd broken up that he'd slept with another girl in my social group. No, this guy was for the streets, he was there for everybody!

As I said, jealousy wasn't a big thing for me back then, so both of these girls got off lightly. I just told them all to fuck off and carried on with my business. If this had happened when I was in my twenties, things would have been different.

These days, I don't have time to fight over men. I'm a grown-arse adult, with a career and a life. I also have a nineteen-year-old daughter who I need to show how to be a woman. I want to encourage her to be her own person and not reliant on men.

I guess all of these experiences were part of a bigger pic-ture, and choosing the right people to trust was something I had to learn the hard way. In those days, I didn't have any real boundaries in place, so I took people at face value. My goal was always just to chill and have fun, so I hung with people who liked to do the same, even if some of them might not have always had my back. I craved normality, and this was my way of getting it. Perhaps that's why my judgement about people, places and things wasn't always as sharp as it might have been, and that's what sometimes landed me in trouble.

In some ways, I still crave that same normality, and like to keep my work life and social life separate. That still works best for me. I don't mix in showbusiness circles and I don't have the phone numbers of celebrities in my contacts. If I see other performers and artists on a night out, I'm always friendly and say hello, but they're not the people I hang out and chill with. The difference between then and now is, I'm much more careful and selective about the people I do spend my time with.

EIGHT

IN JULY 2001, WE RELEASED our fourth single, 'Soul Sound'. In ten months, we'd released 'New Year', 'Run For Cover' and an album, and during that time it had been non-stop. Despite all of our success, we were still young and naive and there were people around us who weren't as helpful and supportive as they might have been. When things got difficult or one of us was struggling, the care and support needed wasn't always there and we were often left to our own devices. It was like that across the industry. We were three headstrong sixteen-year-old girls who had become like sisters in every way – good and bad. While we always cared for one another, and had a great time together while we were performing, the pressures on us sometimes caused personality clashes and arguments. I can only speak for myself, and I was, I suppose, the rebel of the band – more interested in my life outside Sugababes than the day-to-day workings of the band. I'm sure that must have been difficult for the other girls sometimes, and for that reason I guess I ignored some of the cracks that had started to appear during that crazy year. There was always love between us, but outside work we were all still going our own ways, with different groups of friends and separate lives. These days, Siobhan, Keisha and I are very close, and love hanging out together, but back then things were getting more and more fraught as the pressures of the job intensified. It wasn't so much fighting and arguing; it was more that we weren't communicating with one another. We were all experiencing our own shit, but we were pushing down our anxieties and struggles so we could get on with our work.

While we were in Japan doing promotion, a bombshell came from nowhere. At least, that's the way it seemed to me.

It was our first trip to Japan and a real eye-opener. The fact that we were so far away from home but were still being recognized was mind-blowing to me. Even with our obvious success, I couldn't get my head around the fact that people knew who we were outside of the UK. The idea that our music was being played and enjoyed so far away, sometimes by people who didn't even speak English, was beautiful to me.

For me, Tokyo felt like another planet. Its bright, fast-moving landscape was unlike anywhere else I'd ever seen, and even though I've never been back, I remember it all so vividly. The brilliant glow of the city lights, the cutting-edge technology which seemed to be everywhere, and the amazing young fans we met there. Kids with crazy haircuts and dyed-blonde afros, wearing super-trendy clothes. They went nuts every time we appeared, the enthusiasm they had for our music gave us so much energy.

To me, everything seemed to move faster in Tokyo, and it felt like everyone was living life 24/7. We'd get into a glass lift in some high-rise hotel, and I'd look out at people playing tennis, football or basketball late into the night; shopping in the markets or flooding into the karaoke bars. Just thinking about it now makes me desperate to go back again.

When we first arrived, some people from our record label took us to a fantastic sushi restaurant. I love sushi now, but back then I wouldn't have dreamed of eating raw fish. I just sat there, looking down at the table, not quite knowing what to do. I remember just pushing it around my plate for ages! It also didn't help that during that particular meal there was a bloody earthquake in the middle of it. One minute, we were sitting around while one of the guys from the Japanese label sang 'Bohemian Rhapsody' on karaoke, the next we were under the fucking table with the building shaking around us, terrified.

The trip had been gruelling, with fourteen-hour days of back-to-back appearances and interviews. We were all exhausted and it was hot there. So hot! As amazing as the trip had been, we were all feeling out of our comfort zone and a little on edge. One morning, I walked into our dressing room and our manager broke the news that made my head spin.

'Siobhan's gone home. She caught a flight and went back to England.'

Keisha and I looked at one another, baffled. We'd all gone to Japan together, for the same goal, to promote our album. Now one of us had upped and disappeared. We were both totally dumbfounded. We hadn't seen it coming at all. I was so caught up in the whirlwind that I missed a lot of stuff I would have been more aware of today. I was a teenager wrapped up in what I was doing in the moment, and what I might be doing with my friends the next time I saw them. The idea that some-thing as huge as that might have been brewing behind closed doors just didn't cross my mind. I was oblivious.

The worst part about it was that we hadn't even got to see her before she left. There was no warning, so no chance for us to ask her how she felt and why. She'd just disappeared.

More than anything, I felt confused. Suddenly and abruptly, we were packing up and flying home because of this huge and unexpected curveball. No one had properly explained to us what had happened. Siobhan had gone, and at that moment we had no idea what that might mean for us.

I won't go into details about why Siobhan left. That's her story to tell. It was a huge shock, of course, but as a self-absorbed teenager my first thought was, *What will happen to us now?* Will we be able to carry on with our record label and management? Were we still the Sugababes?

When I look back on it, I wish I'd spotted how much Siobhan was struggling. If it were happening now, I'd have picked up on it. I'm older and more sensitive to other people's issues, especially having suffered my fair share. But back then, we were all so caught up in our own stuff it just hadn't occurred to me. It was a confusing and worrying time for the whole team, but being young I don't think I took it as seriously as I could have. I cared about what had happened, but at the same time, my teenage brain was saying, 'So what?' I think it was just youth; we had a lot of resilience and were ready to keep it moving.

The problem was, it wasn't just as simple as us continuing without her. It turned out London Records were dropping Sugababes from the label. One of our management team sprung that one on us once we were back in London. They said it was down to a combination of the split and the fact that *One Touch* hadn't reached the expectations of the label, sales-wise. 'Soul Sound' had only just scraped the top thirty. The news was such a blow. Not only did we have to find a new member, we had to find a new record label if we were going to survive.

I didn't know if we could get through such an explosion of bad shit, and I was worried everything was going to fall apart. We were still only sixteen, and Siobhan's departure was so early in our career. We were out there, yes, but not fully established.

We weren't exactly household names yet, but then maybe that was a good thing if we had to find a new member. It was hard to call it either way.

I later heard that Siobhan was working on solo music, still with London Records. I felt conflicted. I was so happy to know that she was OK, but it was hard knowing that Siobhan had stayed with the label while Keisha and I had been cut.

Our management team didn't seem too concerned about what was to come, and soon after they were organizing auditions for a new third member of the band. The plan was that once we had found a new girl, we would start working on new material. We'd barely recovered from Siobhan's departure when Keisha and I went down to some of the early auditions and saw all these different girls trying out. It felt so weird for me, trying to imagine these people we didn't know coming into something that was well established. We watched one girl after the other, but I wasn't sure if I knew what we were looking for – another Siobhan? Someone who was very different to me, or like me? The way the three of us had come together had been so organic. When we first sang together it just felt right. Auditioning like this didn't feel all that natural. And underneath it all, we were sitting with the knowledge that we didn't even have a deal any more. Whatever happened, this was going to be an uphill struggle.

One of the girls we saw was, of course, Heidi Range. The moment she came in, everyone seemed to sit up and pay attention. Looking back, I think management had already decided Heidi was the one, and the auditions were more of a formality. It was probably a waste of our time. Heidi had been one of the original members of Atomic Kitten, and was under the same management umbrella as us already. When the auditions were over, it was obvious everyone was leaning towards Heidi. It felt like a done deal, and I went along with it because I knew it needed to happen. If we were going to carry on as a group, we had to have someone who could fit in fast and do the job well.

Inside, I worried that Heidi felt quite different to Keisha and me – she was very 'pop' in her approach whereas we'd always been a little unpolished in a way that really worked for us. She also seemed older than us in her mannerisms and approach to things; there was a certain maturity about her. In fact, at one point, I asked if she would show me her passport because I didn't believe she was only eighteen. As weird as it felt to have a new person thrust into the group though, I didn't have an issue with Heidi. We got along very well, and when it came down to it, we all wanted to make this new set-up work. We had to.

The three of us started working on new songs straight away, and not long after we were signed by Island Records. It was a huge relief knowing that we were going to get another crack at the whip, that it wasn't all over. Things took off pretty quickly from there. I think everything happens for a reason, and Heidi's arrival and the slightly more commercial pop vibe we created in the studio with her turned out to be a positive thing. From then on, Sugababes went from strength to strength.

For me, we weren't a better or worse version of the band, just different. Apart from the sound, which was more refined and commercial, Heidi also gave us a different look – she brought Heidi-ness to the group, and it worked. Suddenly, our styling changed. We were made to look less moody and unapproachable, softer perhaps. Kids didn't seem as wary as they once might have been, running over to say hello at signings and appearances. Well, they were still a bit wary of me. Heidi was always the first one they'd go to – she was always so happy and smiley – then it was Keisha. I'd often hang in the background, not wanting to force myself on to some poor child who looked like they were fucking terrified of me. I found it a bit upsetting sometimes. I came from such a big family, with loads of kids who all loved me. Seeing kids who were scared of me made me feel a bit choked. I knew what a caring person I was on the inside – I adored my family, I loved children – but clearly that wasn't coming across on the outside.

In the end, Heidi and Keisha would tell them, 'Go and say hi to Mutya,' and if they were feeling brave, they would. I remember thinking, *Hold tight! I must be doing something wrong here if people can't see who I really am.*

Our first single release with the new line-up was 'Freak Like Me', produced by Richard X. We were working with a fresh sound, with bootleg mash-ups of different style tracks. 'Freak' was a cover of a 1995 track by American R&B singer Adina Howard, but also sampled the 1979 song 'Are "Friends" Electric?' by Gary Numan and Tubeway Army. I knew and loved the original Adina version; in fact, it was one of the songs I'd sometimes sing at Filipino festivals when I was a kid. You'd think knowing the song already would be helpful, but it actually made getting my head around the new mash-up version really hard – it was a bit of a shock. The original was so full of soul, how would people react to this new take on it with its big electro-synth riffs? My mum loved the old Gary Numan stuff, so I also knew that song too. I just wasn't sure they went together. This was the first single of a new Sugababes and it sounded nothing like anything that had come from us before. It certainly didn't sound like anything else that was in the charts at that time. *Was that a good thing, or were people going to be put off?*

It turned out I was worrying for nothing. 'Freak Like Me' debuted at number one in the BBC Top 40 on its release in April 2002. It stayed in the top ten for four weeks and went gold. It was also a huge hit around Europe. The *Guardian* named 'Freak Like Me' the best number-one single of 2002. *NME* called it genius, and, down the line, Billboard had it at number 45 on a list of 100 Greatest Girl Group Songs of All Time.

We already had an audience and a fanbase, but suddenly it was bigger – much bigger – and doors were opening everywhere. Sugababes had been successful before, but it felt different this time. Having a number-one single, and such a defining one, was like having a wind behind us. It gave us momentum and people couldn't wait to see what might come next.

Following 'Freak Like Me', our next single, 'Round Round' – which we co-wrote – also went straight to number one, was certified gold and became a worldwide hit. Whatever we were doing, it was working. A lot of it was down to the writers and producers we worked with at Xenomania, the pop production team headed up by producer Brian Higgins.

I loved working at the studios there. Brian was amazing at what he did and he'd surrounded himself with a great team of people. His way of producing was completely different to anything I'd experienced before. Brian would have several different teams working with us in different rooms, and us girls came up with ideas for verses, bridges and chorus. Then he would take all of those different elements and mix them together to create something quirky and unique. Often, I'd be in one studio while Keisha was in another and Heidi in a third. Sometimes one of us was working on something that sounded totally different to the others, but Brian would fuse the strongest bits together seamlessly. If you listen to a song like 'Round Round', you'll notice that the verses and bridges are very different to one another melodically, and then there's this very slowed-down middle eight section that sounds like it belongs in some other song. You wouldn't naturally put that all together, but somehow it just made sense. This was all because of how Brian's team worked, and why their songs had such a distinct vibe.

Mostly we loved it, but there were times where the vision felt like a stretch, even for us. There's a song on our fourth album, *Taller in More Ways*, called 'Ace Reject', that I remember finding particularly hard to get into. Every section is different and there are lots of little bits that make up the song. For me it felt like we were all singing about slightly different things, so I never saw how it all fitted together and it made it a pain in the arse to remember. It must have been one of our longest tracks; it felt like it went on for ever when we were singing it, so we rarely chose to perform it live. Don't get me wrong, it worked, and people liked it, but to me it just felt like a real mishmash of ideas in one song. Our music was certainly more out there and off-the-wall than some of the simpler tunes in the charts at the time. Even lyrics-wise there were a few lines in our songs where people would listen and go, *Huh?* Sometimes, even I did! With 'Round Round', for instance, I thought for ages that the lyric was, 'we'll ride stir-fried'.

'No,' the girls would tell me. 'It's not bloody stir-fried, Mutya, it's, *still fired*!'

I quite liked working the way we did, often split up while doing our vocals and writing. When you're in among other strong personalities, as we were, with everyone putting their ideas forward, it can sometimes be hard to shine. I'm always quite laid-back when it comes to the studio and tend to go with the flow. If I didn't like something back then, I was never one to speak up and voice that. I didn't want to come across as too opinionated or bitchy. But working separately meant I had the chance to be creative, and stand apart from the other girls. I felt more confident coming up with my own lyrics and melodies and putting them out there. Working by myself, I felt like I could be heard, and that everyone had a voice. My thoughts and ideas weren't just swallowed in a wave of other opinions.

That time felt like a special moment for pop music. The industry felt really close-knit and many of us artists socialized together. I would often see Gareth Gates or members of Girls Aloud, Blue or Busted out in the bars and clubs. It was almost guaranteed that if you went out on any given night of the week in London, you'd see people you knew from the entertainment industry. I was fortunate in that I got along with pretty much everyone. Well, that's not completely true – with that many personalities, there's always going to be a bit of drama. I had a few minor tiffs with a couple of the girls from Atomic Kitten. Liz was always lovely, but for some reason I felt that Natasha and Jenny did not like me.

There were a few comments back and forth over time, but I tried to let it all wash over me. I guess we were all a lot younger and less mature back then, and I could certainly give attitude when I wanted to. Maybe it was just that era. There was often a competitive spirit, which sometimes turned to bitchiness between bands. The media didn't help either – they thrived on the drama. Things feel very different now, and it makes me laugh thinking back on how caught up we all got in our own silly rows. In fact, I saw Natasha from Atomic Kitten recently and we hugged, kissed and caught up.

For the most part, though, I had a very good rapport with my fellow artists. The vibes were great because we all saw so much of one another. If you weren't out socializing, you were hanging out together backstage at roadshows or in TV studios. Dressing-room doors were always open, and everyone would gather in corridors and green rooms. There was never a dull moment! It wasn't just the artists themselves either. You'd get to know people who worked for various record labels or behind the scenes at the studios. It felt like one big community. At the end of 2023, we performed on *Jools Holland's Annual Hootenanny* and I recognized one of the BBC cameramen, who used to be behind the cameras back in the day when we were doing *Top of the Pops* and *CD:UK*. I thought, *God, we were all a hundred years younger back then* – well, twenty-three years younger anyway! It sometimes feels like a lifetime ago.

It's funny how vivid and exciting memories of that era feel to me now. At the time, I took everything in my stride to the point of indifference. I wouldn't say I was unappreciative of the life I had, but I was sort of unaware of its magnitude. So much of it passed me by in a blur and I wish I had been more present. I wish I'd taken it in and enjoyed the band's success – my success! I feel like I often missed out on really revelling in those champagne-popping moments and number-one highs. It was a case of, *Yeah, cheers, thanks, now let's get on with it!* I didn't acknowledge what we had. Maybe because we started so young, it just felt 'normal'. I suppose I didn't really know any different.

These days, I thank God every day for what I've got and for

all that I've done. I'm fortunate that I get to remember and even relive some of those fantastic moments with Keisha and Siobhan now, every time we step out on stage. But I sometimes wish I could turn back time – just so I could pat myself on the back and celebrate, well, me!

NINE

AT SEVENTEEN, I MOVED OUT of my home and into a town-house with three women in their twenties. At the time, a lot of my friends were a couple of years older than me, and I worked with so many adults that I figured that I could live with older girls too. I knew two of them quite well from going out and about together. They were moving into a nice house and there was a room going spare, so I thought, *Why not?*

It wasn't like I didn't have freedom already. Being in the band, travelling the world and clubbing all over central London – I was already doing my own thing – but the idea of having my own place was a step on from that. As me and my siblings all got older, and various girlfriends and boyfriends started coming around, the flat was feeling a lot more cramped. In many ways, I was getting the best of both worlds. The new place was a ten-minute walk from my family home, so while I was getting my own space, Mum and Dad were still close at hand if and when I needed them. I don't think they were that keen on me moving out – they'd probably have preferred it if I'd stayed at home a little longer – but knowing how independent I was, they didn't say much about it. I was a stubborn teenager, earning her own money and very sure of what she wanted. So, aside from letting me know they were always there for me, my parents went along with my decision to step out on my own.

Unlike me, my new housemates all had what you might call 'regular' jobs. Davina worked the door of a club and Corrine worked for Brent Council. We all got on well, and while the third girl tended to do her own thing, the rest of us hung out together as much as we could and became close. My schedule with the band was still crazy, but now, the rare time I had to myself truly was my own. I could do whatever I wanted without my parents or brothers having a say. Sometimes, Corrine would pick me up in her convertible and we would go out, driving around town and having fun. For me, that felt like the point where my life really began, and there were good times to be had. My memories of that house are tinged with nostalgia and warmth. I loved cooking, so the place was always well stocked with food, and you'd often find me in the kitchen, a glass of wine in one hand, a spoon in the other, whipping up something tasty. The vibe in that house was always nice.

Being slightly older, the other girls looked after me to an extent – as much as I would let them. My family were still very much a part of my life too.

We might not have been under the same roof, but being so local meant that I'd often have my brothers and their mates around, and, of course, there were lots of spur-of-the-moment gatherings and house parties. There was one party I threw – I can't for the life of me remember what the occasion was – when the whole of the boy band Blazing Squad turned up. All ten of them. They were cool guys, and that night they got along with my brothers and their friends like a house on fire.

Naturally, during those years, if I wasn't working or out clubbing, I'd be at a local pub with my housemates and our extended group of friends. The bonus to staying local was that I still knew a lot of people, so there was always someone to chill with. Far from the girl that was so isolated after leaving school, I finally felt like I had found my people. And with that, my appetite for going out and having fun just grew and grew.

With the 'new' Sugababes flying, I was well into my cycle of partying from Monday to Sunday while working a full schedule. Back then, nobody told me I shouldn't be doing it, and because they all still wanted and needed me, I saw no reason to stop. I couldn't have known it at the time, but this was the start of me slowly destroying myself. Still only a teenager, I didn't see it like that, and why would I? I was having a great time and wasn't having to face any consequences. My head was telling me, *This is what I want to do right now.* So why on earth would I stop?

I think about how I am now with my own daughter, who's nineteen – I'm all over her. If she's out and it's close to midnight, I'll message her to ask what time she'll be home. I didn't have that at her age or even younger, and that's not because my parents didn't care: they just knew they'd be fighting a losing battle. I probably wouldn't have listened to them telling me to come home early or even answered their phone call, especially since I'd moved out of the family home. I was having a good time, the best time, and that was all that mattered.

'Mutya's gone missing' was a hot phrase around that time, but it happened so often that everyone started to get used to it. If I was off for three days at a time, going from club to club, or chilling at somebody's house after hours, everyone got on with their lives, knowing I would eventually turn up and carry on where I'd left off. If any other girl my age had gone AWOL for days at a time, the police would have been called, and they'd be on the missing persons list. With me, it got to the point where everyone knew I was out partying and that I'd come home when I was good and ready. Of course, friends and family members might text or call me while I was off having fun; sometimes they'd get an answer, and sometimes they wouldn't. It was always a gamble, and there was no big panic if I didn't respond. I always rocked up sooner or later and most of the time I got on with whatever I had to do as normal.

I don't know what Keisha and Heidi thought of my other life. If they talked about it together, I never heard anything. That's not to say they weren't there for me if I was feeling low: they were always patient. I just reckon, like everybody else, by then they were used to my various ups and downs.

There were times when I was feeling tired or hungover at work, and I'd think, *You should have been at home in bed last night.* There were even points on nights out, often in the early hours, when I'd think, *How much more can I do of this?* My answer always came quickly: *Well, I'm still fucking young, so a lot more.* My mantra was: *It's fine, you deserve to let your hair down.* The trouble was, I was telling myself that every single day.

On rough mornings-after I was often more withdrawn, maybe smoking a spliff or just not saying much at all. It was the only way I knew to get through the day before heading out again. I didn't really consider other people's thoughts and opinions on the matter. Sometimes, I could kick myself, looking back on it. Other times I want to give eighteen-year-old me a hug and tell her she's all right.

It was a miracle my partying didn't get me into more hot water with the press, but luckily for me, I was out with people who weren't interested in the limelight. Nobody around me cared what I was doing, they just wanted to have fun! Maybe that was why the girls never voiced their opinions on my other life. It was never in the public domain so maybe they didn't realize how bad it had become.

As time went on, I became pretty experimental too, up for basically anything if it sounded like fun. My adventurous, addictive personality meant that once I got an idea in my head, I felt compelled to see it through. Consequently, I'd find myself in raves and strip clubs of all kinds. I found the experiences freeing, especially coming from a background where my dad had once been quite strict and protective of me, and my brothers even more so. Now, I was out there doing my own thing, and if I couldn't find anyone to party with on a particular night, I'd take off on my own – which wasn't always a good idea.

There was a period around that time when I was always getting into fights with random girls I didn't even know. I seemed to be a magnet for people who felt they had something to prove and decided they needed to take me down a peg or two because of who I was. It was bullying, pure and simple, but I was no pushover.

I could be standing there minding my own business and some smart-mouth drunk girl would decide she couldn't pass by without commenting. The words I remember hearing most were, 'Just because . . .' That was always their opening phrase, and it got to the point where I could finish their sentences for them. 'Just because you think you're famous . . .' 'Just because you're in the Sugababes . . .' Some ended up with a mouthful; others who pushed it weren't so lucky and had to pick themselves up off the floor while I got another drink. I never considered myself a fighter, but there was a year when I felt like I did nothing but fight girls in bars, clubs or at parties. It was relentless.

I think that was when my anxiety and depression really started to rear its head. I began questioning and doubting myself, constantly telling myself that everything was going to go wrong for me. That the worst was going to happen. The voice in my head was taking over and ruling the roost, compelling me to believe every word it said and leaving me with a constant sense of dread that would grow over time. This was just the start of it, and with my partying getting wilder, things were about to get worse.

TEN

ALTHOUGH I DRANK A LOT, I'd always been against hard drugs. I didn't like the idea of them and wasn't interested in trying any. In fact, I could be quite judgemental about people who did, and I certainly saw a lot of it around me.

Things changed at a party when someone I was hanging with said, 'Well, you shouldn't keep knocking it and putting other people down until you've tried it yourself.'

They had happened to catch me in a 'fuck it' moment, and I decided to give it a go. It didn't feel like I was making some big life-changing decision or that it could lead to anything problematic. It was just something I was going to try in that moment at that party. I was still in control. No big deal.

That night, I took my first party drug and I liked how it made me feel – the rush of extra confidence, the feeling that everything and everyone was all right. After that night, and that first time, my fear evaporated, so I did it again . . . and then again . . . until it was a regular thing for me on a night out.

I wish I could say that I was one of those people who could do a little now and then on the odd weekend and then forget about it. There were people around me that seemed to manage that way. I was the opposite. I had an addictive personality and an all-or-nothing attitude. I went from being fairly clean to extremely messy in a flash. At the house raves I went to, there were, of course, always other things on offer. I was dropping a pill, or throwing god knows what in my drink. It was all there for the taking and I took it. Thinking about it now, I can't even say I have regrets about trying those things. Experimentation is all part of growing up. It's not something I would recommend for everyone, but it's part of my story and part of what made me who I am. I just wish I'd been safer.

As my appetite for the wilder side of life grew, it drew me away from the glitz and glamour of the West End clubs to the much darker side of the party scene. At times, I ended up at raves in squats, where some of the guests looked like they hadn't left the fucking place for a hundred years, let alone seen daylight. There seemed to be a long, endless chain of these parties. I'd go to an all-night rave on a Friday evening and then I'd leave and go to another which started at eight a.m. on Saturday. That one would go on till midnight, then there would be another that went on all day Sunday. There was one place I used to frequent, Ghost, which didn't open till seven a.m. If I was being 'good', I'd go to bed the night before, then get up at seven, get there for eight, and stay till midnight before heading to another. Sometimes I'd have already been up all night before I even got there, but I'd still manage to carry on through. Writing about those lost weekends now, I'm thinking, *You dirty bitch! You must have gone so long without having a wash or cleaning your teeth!*

I have no idea how I had it in me to do this while still managing to somehow function during my busy working life. With hindsight, I probably thought I was handling things a lot better than I actually was. As far as I was concerned, as long as I got the job done, all was right with the world, and I had no reason to calm down my night-time activities. I thought I was carrying on with work like a pro, but I reckon the people who had to deal with me at the time might say differently.

The blessing and the curse of being me at that time was that I wasn't scared of anything. I'd go anywhere and try anything without fear. Early morning or the middle of the night, if the mood took me I'd get up and go – in search of something. The next buzz, the next bit of fun. Often, I'd get lost in that adventure and go missing for days, losing track of time and myself. Sometimes, I'd be drifting around not knowing where I was or who I was with. In a lucid moment, I might think, *Whose house am I at now? How did I get here?*

Sometimes that newfound bravery landed me in situations that weren't so safe. Those underground raves often brought trouble. On more than one occasion, I was chased by the police because of incidents I'd witnessed or been in the vicinity of. I did see people get hurt, a lot. When it happened, I wanted to get out of the place as soon as I could, but that wasn't always possible. Sometimes, I'd get stuck in there for hours because fights had broken out and we wanted to keep out of the way. One time, I ended up trapped in a bathroom with some friends, barricading the door because a huge brawl was raging on the other side of it. For some reason, people loved to drop my name while they were being interviewed by the police, even though the incident had nothing to do with me. Maybe it was because I was recognizable, or because mine was the only name they knew, but it happened. It meant that I was always being tracked down for questioning.

Over time, I had the police turning up at my mum's house, at my house, and even calling my management or my parents.

Whenever they caught up with me, I would insist I'd been there to party and that any violence was nothing to do with me. They always believed me, but after a while I started getting tired of hearing my name come up.

'If you don't want us chasing you down, maybe you should start going to different places, because people keep calling your name out,' one policeman told me.

This was when I'd been summoned to court to give evidence in a case. I didn't know anything and I didn't want to go, but the policeman was threatening me with all sorts if I didn't show.

'How would you feel if you got hurt and no one wanted to come forward?' he said.

He had a point, and I should've listened to his advice, but at the time I wasn't thinking straight. The whole thing had shaken me, but also brought into brutal focus the fact that I was living two completely different lives in parallel: the pop life, where I was styled and photographed and ferried around in cars, and the party life, where I was being chased down by the cops.

I wish I could tell you that it put me off going to those parties, but it didn't. As awful as some of those things were, I was numb to the danger; I felt invincible. Perhaps I thought it was just all part and parcel of going out. As far as I was concerned, I was only there to enjoy myself with my friends and, despite some of the bad things that happened, I never knowingly walked into a place where I didn't feel safe. I knew a lot of people and was generally around a bunch of friends and acquaintances who would look after me. The naivety that got me into danger when I was younger was still there in many ways, and I was oblivious to just how much trouble I could get into if I wasn't more careful.

Even my holidays were based around getting wasted. I'd go to Ibiza, Aya Napa – the party islands, of course – with a group of my girlfriends, many of whom I'm still friends with to this day. These trips were full-on banging weeks of hedonism where I'd lose my mind and my soul, but I usually managed to get on the plane and be back at work when I was needed. Notice how I say 'usually'! There was more than one occasion when I'd be on Bora Bora beach club waving at the plane that I was supposed to be on as it flew over. I think I cancelled my plane home three or four times because I couldn't tear myself away from the island. My soul was stuck there.

On those trips, I'd always end up meeting fun groups of people. I was a magnet for stag dos – guys on bachelor weekends would always find me and I'd end up joining in the fun, whatever they were up to! I'd find myself in villas, jumping into pools half-naked, thinking I could swim, only to realize once I'd hit the water that I couldn't. There was never a sexual element; I was just one of the lads, joining them at a bar or at their table for dinner. Sometimes, I'd end up in a villa in the hills somewhere with these randoms that I hadn't known twenty-four hours ago. Essex boys, Manchester lads . . . I was always in the midst of it! I never had to pay for anything and I was having the time of my life. And no matter what crazy, over-the-top fun I was having, they always looked after me.

Thank God that was the case. I didn't know those people, and I could have walked into any kind of situation. Many people go to Ibiza to enjoy fun and decadent times, but I was always ready to take things a step further. The party drugs were usually flowing freely, and wherever I was, it was all about that kind of indulgence.

One night, while staying at a villa with some friends, I was in my room, in deep conversation, when one of my friends popped their head round the door.

'You coming out of there?' she said.

'In a minute,' I said.

'Who are you talking to anyway?' she said.

I suddenly realized I was alone. I'd been having a long, in-depth conversation with nobody. Seconds after that, I thought I was staring into the eyes of the grim reaper, who I was convinced had arrived to bring me to the afterlife. I recall having a fleeting thought that if I was going to die, I might as well do it in Ibiza. For me, the White Island always meant freedom. If I felt stressed or needed to blow off steam, that was where I wanted to be.

During a time when I was, let's say, experimental, as far as partying went, my dad always called me a daredevil, and he was right. I never thought twice about doing or taking anything within reason. I've never tried heroin or crack, but all the other Ibiza party favours were on the table. Jesus, I couldn't do it now; I love my sleep too much! Back then, however, I barely knew what sleep was. My motto then was 'Sleep when you're dead!' I never wanted to regret *not* doing something. And that's how things stayed for a long time. It was, for me, the good life, whereas nowadays the good life is eating good food and sleeping.

There reached a point, however, when even I could see that it had become too much. The practical part of me poked its head up and made a decision. I banned myself from Ibiza for ten years. I couldn't trust myself to go there and not go absolutely crazy. I felt like there was a real possibility that it was the place I was going to die. So, much as I loved it, the White Island was out of the picture.

These days, when I go on holidays with the girls, it's not the party islands we're in search of, it's quieter, more exotic locations. We're looking for different kinds of fun. Now, it's about lazing by the pool, sunbathing, sipping cocktails, getting dressed up at night and heading out for beautiful dinners at fabulous restaurants. I'm not even looking to get drunk, let alone anything else! If only I'd known back then that I didn't need drugs to have an amazing time.

ELEVEN

SLOWLY, THE SMALL AMOUNT OF control I felt I had over my partying started to slip away. One night, I had a traumatic experience that changed me for ever. At the time I was renting an apartment in west London with some friends, and being so close to central London meant that the clubs were even more accessible to me than they had ever been. During that time, there had been nights when I'd blacked out, those evenings totally lost to me. I couldn't remember what I'd done because of the alcohol and drugs I'd consumed. It was alarming, but didn't really put me off. That was until one morning when I woke up to severe pains in my arm. For a few minutes, trying to drag myself back into consciousness, I couldn't figure out what was going on, just that it hurt badly. I sat up and looked around the room, realizing I'd spent the night on the living-room sofa while everyone else had gone to bed. My eyes flicked from a bloody knife on the floor to deep cuts on my arm, which were still bleeding. What the fuck had happened? Had someone done this to me? Had I done it to myself? Surely not. I'd never seen anyone self-harm or thought about doing it. Why would I suddenly have picked up a knife and sliced chunks out of my arm? I was scared at the thought but had a nasty feeling that was what had happened. I couldn't think of any other explanation.

I went upstairs and woke my friends; I had a lot of questions.

Why did they all go up to bed without waking me? Why did nobody think to come down and check on me? Surely I must've been in a bad way to end up at this point? Nobody had any answers. But I don't suppose they could've known what was coming that night, given how things were with me at the time. I was left with the confusing realization that I had self-harmed. And I couldn't even remember it. I wondered what must have been going on below the surface to take me to that place. I was having a good time, living my life as I wanted. I had a successful career in music and had what I felt was a fantastic, fun, social life. So why?

After that night, it happened again; only this time, I knew what I was doing. I wish I could tell you how it went from being something alien to me to a conscious and deliberate action, but I just don't know. I guess being tough on the outside meant that I was pushing all the hurt inside. When you hear and read negative things about yourself all the time, it's impossible not to start believing some of them deep down. After years of swallowing my pride and trying to ignore the criticism that came almost daily from the press and the public, my dislike of myself really grew. The only way I felt I could control it was to blast it with alcohol and other stuff. When that stopped doing the trick, self-harm came to me as another option.

From then on, whenever I felt pushed to my limits or like I couldn't breathe, I'd turn to this. Soon, it became a regular thing. If I was angry, frustrated or upset, hurting myself became my way of releasing all that. In a confrontational situation or argument, I would tell people, 'Don't push me, please don't push me,' because I knew where it would lead.

The sad, undeniable truth was that I hated myself. In fact, there wasn't a single part of me I celebrated or enjoyed. It's hard to pinpoint where that started, but years in the limelight have a tendency to morph into a deep insecurity. I'd hidden it from myself for years but suddenly it was there – a presence in the room I couldn't ignore.

I went down a dark path, and for whatever reason, I felt I needed to punish myself. As painful as it was for me, there was a relief in doing it. That's how fucked up my head was. I found comfort in it. It felt like something I could control, something that could relieve the pressure. When I felt overly stressed or upset with life, when I felt bricks on my shoulders, it was my go-to. Most people have their own way of escaping from their problems and stresses, but while someone else might go to the gym or to the pub, self-harming was my way. It was extreme, but then again, so was my life at the time. The trouble is, when I was deep in the midst of it, I'd forget what the aftermath would be. It felt right at the time, but straight after came the cold moment of clarity: the pain, the shame, the embarrassment of having to cover up my secret when I had a show to do and a stage outfit to choose. Still, I'd reached a point where I didn't care about all that. Whenever people were pushing me or pressuring me, that was where I was going – whatever the consequences might be.

Eventually, people around me, some friends and family members, realized what was happening and confronted me about it. I'd try to tell them that they wouldn't understand. How could I explain to them that shutting the curtains and hurting myself was like a breath of fresh air to me? It was a relief, that torture. I didn't have the answers as to why, but I knew it to be true.

There were times when I sat in the dark for days at a time, not wanting to eat or speak to anyone, locking myself away from the world. Some days, my sleep patterns were so off, I'd sleep all day, then wake up, thinking it was morning and wondering why it was dark.

There was less understanding of self-harm back then. If people heard you were doing something as drastic as that, they thought you were fucking nuts.

Things got darker still on the photo shoot for the *Angels with Dirty Faces* album, our second, in Spain. I'd been taking antidepressants at the time, but for some reason I didn't take them with me on the trip, and I was suffering without them.

We were shooting by a lake in blazing sunshine, and it felt like a hundred degrees, so I wasn't overly pleased when the stylist on the shoot stuck me in a polo-neck top. I noticed with envy that Keisha and Heidi were much more suitably dressed for scorching weather, and as the shoot went on, I got more down about the situation. I felt I wasn't being treated fairly, and that thought grew. It bubbled away in my head, making me more and more pissed off. The trouble was, I didn't speak up; I just suffered in silence, seething and simmering about it, getting more and more paranoid about a relatively small thing. *Why was I being covered up when they weren't? Was I too fat? Did I not look as good as the other girls? Why are they dressing me like a nun?*

Keisha and Heidi could see what I was doing to myself. By now, the girls were used to talking me down from situations when I was mad at the world. I just wasn't always good at hearing them. It was never any use reassuring me that things would be OK because, in my head, things would only be OK when *I* said they were.

Once I started to overthink things, it was almost impossible for me or anyone else to bring me back. It was like my head was exploding, and there was no stopping it. That was what happened that day under the baking sun. The simmering thoughts boiled over.

In the end, I walked away from the shoot and called my management.

'I need to see a doctor,' I said. 'I need to get some antidepressant tablets.'

'Can it wait till after the shoot?' they asked me.

'No, I need to see a doctor as soon as possible.'

Someone found a private doctor who prescribed me some pills so we could go on with the shoot. It's probably the worst thing I could have done. As some of you probably know, antidepressants are not something that work instantly. It's not like a headache tablet where you take it and the pain disappears in a few minutes. The doctor's advice was to take one if I was feeling low, but when I realized that one tablet wasn't cutting it, I took another and another, desperate for an immediate result. I was taking them in the loo and I didn't realize how strong they were. In the end, I was popping them like crazy until everything went black. I collapsed during the shoot. I see now I should've told the crew I was taking them, but I didn't think it would be an issue.

The next thing I remember is coming back into consciousness somewhere noisy. It's a cliché, but for a moment, it was like I was looking down on myself, lying in a hospital bed. I felt like I was taking in the scene from above, and I could hear people saying my name but couldn't answer. When I came round fully, I was bruised all over, had a tube down my throat and was wondering what the fuck had happened. I was so scared at that moment that I pulled at the tube and went berserk at the

My dad with baby me, his Princess Pearl.

Tiny Mutya, in a classic 80s jacket I would
probably still wear today.

Me, with three of my big brothers. From left to right: Kris, Roberto and Danny.

Big sis Mutya, always looking out for her little sisters. Ligaya (left) and Dalisay (right).

Winning first place at one of the many competitions I entered as a child. I was always up against children much older than me!

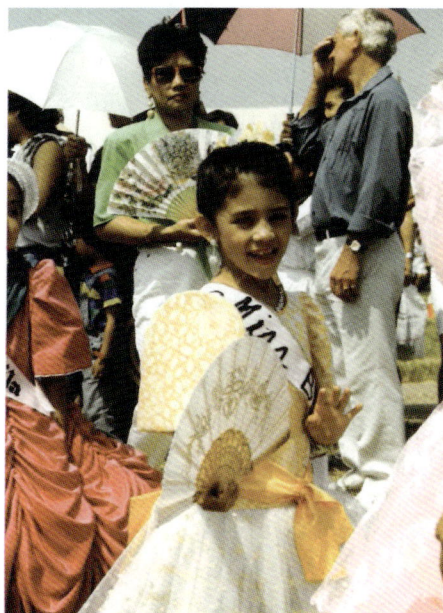

Two classic examples of my Little Miss Philippines pageant outfits: all frills and glitter – I was like a walking meringue!

Hiding from the camera in my childhood bedroom. You can see the posters of my favourite musicians and, of course, the Philippines that I plastered all over my walls!

In the Philippines with my hair clipped up, just before I finally won the battle to get it cut short for the first time.

Singing at a classic Filipino function back in the day. You can see the book of songs I'd flip through to pick my next track.

Sugar babies! These are some of our early looks – I can't believe how
tiny we all were!

At the MOBOs in 2007, where I was nominated for 'Best Newcomer' after the release of my solo album. Little did I know that almost twenty years later I'd be back there as part of Sugababes again, receiving the Impact award.

Performing solo at V Festival in 2007. It felt so scary being onstage by myself after being part of a trio for so long.

Me and Tahlia at the gala performance of *The Sponge Who Could Fly* in 2009.
One of my favourite things about my job was being able to take her to wacky
things like this!

Like mother, like daughter!

Then and now. The OG lineup of Sugababes at the Brit awards in 2001 and in 2025. So blessed to have grown up with these girls, and so proud of how far we've come.

nurses, screaming and shouting at them to let me up. It took hospital security coming in with batons to restrain me. The fear had me acting crazy. I had no idea where I was or how I got there.

I don't know why I did what I did that day. I certainly hadn't been trying to end my life, but at the same time, I clearly didn't know how to deal with what I was feeling.

Thinking about it now feels strange. From what I've been told, I was close to dying that day. In fact, from what I heard later, they thought they'd lost me at one point. It's one of the many things I never talk about because I've pushed it out of my mind, as people often do with traumatic experiences. I was always good at that – pushing things away and then forgetting they'd ever happened. I don't like to think about how close I was to the edge.

With big highs, there are always lows. I could no longer ignore the downside of my partying as the fear and paranoia began to creep in during the comedowns. In the early days, I bounced from one high to another, but as I began to struggle more with my mental health it became harder to feel 'normal' the morning after. One of the areas where this became really obvious was travel. We were busy across Europe so were constantly on the go, but jumping on planes every week really brought out my anxiety. When I was coming down off the ceiling after being out all weekend, I just wanted to be at home on my sofa with the lights low, phone off and curtains closed, not up in the sky with a ton of people. On days like this, every bump, shake and movement of the plane got me worked up to the point where I was terrified of crashing. In the end, I was so convinced I was going to die every time I took a flight, I'd have to drink a fair bit of alcohol before I got on the plane. Sometimes I would even pop a few pills, just to calm me down. That's how bad it was.

Eventually, that side of things seemed to be massively out-weighing the good times. A hangover seemed like a reasonable price to pay for a good night out, but now it had gone too far. I was no longer flying under the radar. No longer getting the job done. My management were very concerned. Although they found me a handful, more than anything they wanted to help me. A lot of people, both friends and family, reached out to me, but I wasn't good at accepting support. I wasn't an easy person to help.

At one point, my management sat me down for a serious conversation, but I don't recall it having much of an impact. Anyone could have told me I needed a kick up the arse, that I needed help, but I would have told them to fuck off. I'd have told them, and probably did, that I was enjoying myself. And the truth of it was, for most of it, I was. I was having the time of my life. I just couldn't see the toll it was taking.

Drink, drugs, depression and anxiety. By this point I'd built up quite a checklist. Together these things did not make a pretty picture, but when someone doesn't know when to stop, there's only a certain amount of shit the people around you can take. Being the proud girl I am, I always thought I knew best. Eventually, I stopped taking my antidepressants because I decided I could overcome my depression on my own. I didn't need doctors telling me what I needed and I didn't need pills either. What good would they be in the long run anyway? As far as I was concerned, my body would end up getting used to the medication and it would cease to have an effect. After that, I'd just be left to deal with it on my own anyway. No one agreed with me, but at that point they could see I was past help.

It can be frustrating to watch someone you love ignore your advice over and over. Right or wrong, I knew best. There was no changing my mind.

Ultimately, if there was ever to be change, it was going to be down to me to pick myself up and be a better person – whatever that meant!

TWELVE

I MET JAY WHEN I was seventeen or eighteen through a mutual acquaintance. A couple of years older than me, he was a kind and good-looking guy who ran a clothing shop in east London. We started out as friends, but over time, we grew closer and more intimate.

I'd tried to keep details about our relationship out of the press, but reporters and photographers were always trying to figure out if I was dating anyone at the time. Once they clocked that we were together quite often, they were like dogs with a bone. They'd turn up on his mum's estate and parade around it all day, desperate to get a picture of us together.

In early summer 2004, I started feeling sick all the time. Even while I was out having fun, I felt queasy. Around late June or early July, I went to Marbella with some girlfriends, and that's when I really knew something was off. We were all dressed up to the nines at a bar, about to do some shots, when I started feeling a bit odd. Me being me, I still did the shot but then immediately threw up right there in the middle of the bar. My friends all stared at me as if I was an alien, and then one of them said what they were all thinking: 'You're not pregnant, are you?'

'No, I'm not pregnant,' I said, brushing it off. 'Let's get another drink!'

As the holiday continued, we sunbathed and dipped in the pool, but I just couldn't face alcohol, which, for me, was fucking weird. As the days went on, I felt more and more sick, and then I started to think, *Hang on, maybe they're on to something.*

Sure enough, when I got home and did a test, it was confirmed: I was pregnant. I was not in any way ready to be a mother. I was nineteen years old and Sugababes were poised to have a great year. We were gearing up to record our fourth studio album, following up from our two-time platinum album, *Three,* the previous year.

At the time, the thought of being pregnant was the most stressful thing imaginable. Having kids hadn't even crossed my mind at that stage in my life.

I told Jay, of course, but I didn't give him much of a say about what we might do, and I probably should have. As far as I was concerned, and as scary as it all was, I was having this baby with or without him. True, I was worried about being too young and still wanting to enjoy my freedom, but another part of me loved the idea of becoming a mum. I'd grown up in a big family, and always enjoyed being around my friends' babies, pushing their prams and imagining what it might feel like to have a child of my own one day. That day had just come sooner than I'd thought! If Jay didn't want to be a part of it, I'd already decided I would go it alone and bring our child up by myself. In fact, with my tendency to expect the worst, I think I'd convinced myself that was what was going to happen. As it turned out, Jay was cool about becoming a dad, and we decided we were going to make it work as a couple. The idea that we were going to share parenting together was a huge relief.

Without a shred of a doubt, the worst thing about discovering I was pregnant was the thought of telling my dad, because it would mean that he would know I'd had sex. The same went for telling my brothers. That might sound weird given my age, but for me it was a big thing. My brothers were still overly protective of me, and as far as my dad was concerned, I was still his little princess. He'd hate the thought of me even kissing a boy, let alone doing anything else!

As I was gearing up to tell my family, I got very sick.

I was at my parents' house, and had just told my mum about the baby. Mum has always been my saviour, so I could trust her with my news. She's the person I've always been able to be most honest with. Still, even she had mixed emotions when I told her. Like me, she was worried about how we were going to break the news to my dad, but I think she was also worried about how it might affect my career. So was I.

That evening, we ordered Chinese food, but I didn't feel well enough to eat. At one point, I drank a glass of water and felt a stabbing pain in my stomach. Within seconds, I was throwing the water back up. When that subsided slightly, I tried eating something, but the pain returned with a vengeance. As quickly as the food went down, it came up again. Within a couple of minutes, I was rolling around on the carpet in absolute agony, feeling very scared. Mum called an ambulance, which soon arrived to take me to hospital.

It turned out I had a severe kidney infection, and I found myself delirious and on a drip for several days. I couldn't eat or drink. At times, I felt like I was dying. It would have been bad enough at any time but being pregnant made it even more distressing.

I ended up staying in hospital for two weeks and had gone from eight and a half stone to six and half. All that time in a hospital bed gave me a lot of time to overthink, and I was convinced a lot of the illness was brought on by the stress I felt because of my situation. The pregnancy had thrown up so many deep concerns. Aside from the worry of telling the men in my family that I was sexually active, I was also anxious about how Heidi, Keisha and the record label would react. It was obviously going to affect my work and career, but it would affect theirs too.

One day, Mum came in to see me and said the thing I didn't want to hear.

'Bloody hell, Mutya, now we'll have to tell your dad you're pregnant.'

'No, Mum, please, don't!'

In the end, she told my brother Danny, who was the scariest one of all when it came to being overprotective of me. When Mum handed me her phone, with Danny on the line, I was petrified, thinking he was going to be furious. What he said was a big surprise.

'I know and I'm here for you. We're all behind you. Whatever you choose to do, we'll support you.'

For me, there was never really a question of whether I'd have my baby or not, but I was happy and relieved to hear him say that. It turned out I'd been worrying for ages for no reason, because everyone had already figured it out!

When my dad eventually found out, he was more concerned that I might ruin my life and my career than anything else. In the end, though, even he came round. There were already grandkids in the family, and ultimately, he was just happy at the idea of becoming a granddad again.

Around that time, Mum and Dad decided to move to the Philippines to the family house we had there. Dad went first, with Mum planning to follow. One of the main reasons for the move was Mum's health. She'd had problems for some time, with pain in her legs and various other ailments. She always felt so much better when she was there – the sun and the water on the islands nourish her; she eats better and is generally more healthy. It's like she's a whole different person, living a completely different lifestyle. It would be hard to see them go, and the thought of being a new mother without my own mum around scared me, but I had so many other things going on.

At the time, I was still full-on busy with Sugababes. Even with these huge things going on in my life, the schedule never let up. There's a picture of us at the 2005 Brit Awards, me with a large baby bump, and another with the three of us and Amy Winehouse. That year, our track 'In The Middle' was nominated for Best British Single, and we were just starting on our album *Taller in More Ways*.

The girls were so happy for me, and very supportive. In fact, Keisha seemed so over the moon about my pregnancy you'd have thought she was the proud mummy, while I was still getting used to the idea of having a baby. She was always very loving as an auntie to Tahlia, and is to this day – sometimes sharing memories of the time Tahlia was in my belly or when she was little. Their auntie–niece relationship is something beautiful to behold. Even the press stories about my pregnancy were nice – at least the ones I read were! So, as much as the situation had started out with uncertainty and worry, everything seemed to be ticking along nicely. Amid all that joy, however, things were about to change dramatically.

It was around this time that I bought my very first house. Now we were starting a family, it made sense to have a place to call my own. Jay and I moved in together, along with two dogs, Blue and Ice. We shared a love of dogs and loved having them bounding around the house, so much so, that soon after, I added to the family with a chow-chow called Shizzle.

Unfortunately, not long after we'd moved into the house, something truly awful happened.

Jay had a brother who he was very close to, who was really chuffed about becoming an uncle. In fact, he told me at a New Year's gathering at the end of 2004 just how much he looked forward to meeting Tahlia. In early 2005, Jay and I were at home when Jay got a phone call from a woman called Sarah, his mother's neighbour. Sarah told him the news that there had been a terrible incident. He was now on his way to the hospital, badly injured.

We were both in shock, and I drove Jay to the hospital straight away. By that time, I was heavily pregnant, so I dropped him off and came home, waiting for news.

Not long afterwards, the call came to tell me his brother had passed away. Jay was devastated. Thinking about the last time I'd seen him at New Year, I felt so distraught; he'd been so excited about being an uncle. He'd even thoughtfully brought me a glass of Ribena because I couldn't drink alcohol. It was all so unbelievably tragic. He was only twenty-four years old.

I worked right up until the baby was expected, stopping just two weeks before my due date in March 2005. As well as the kidney infection, the rest of my pregnancy was pretty awful too. I was sick for the whole nine months. I threw up every day. Every new smell – smoke, alcohol, certain foods – would turn my stomach. I'm sure a lot of mothers will know how that feels. The funny thing is, my mum had nine children and hadn't throw up at all. I think I got her whole share: nine kids' worth of vomiting with my one baby. Still, there were positive things too. Needless to say, I stopped drinking while I was pregnant, and that in turn helped reset my relationship with alcohol, at least for a while. I still went out a bit, especially at the start, but I was sensible. I guess some of the people with me must have wondered why, when there was a drink or a shot in front of me, I wasn't touching it, but my closest friends were in the know, so knew not to push alcohol my way. If it was a work or promotional thing and someone gave me a bottle, I'd quickly hand it over to one of my friends.

I was booked in at Edgware Hospital to give birth, which was where I'd been born, but when my waters broke a few days before my due date, the hospital didn't have any beds, so I was told I was being sent to another one further away. I wasn't happy with this. There had been reports that a couple of mothers had recently died giving birth at the hospital in question, so I put my foot down and said no. This all happened on the day Mum flew out to the islands to join my dad, which wasn't ideal. She was upset about missing the birth of her grandchild, but she had to do what was right for her.

Meanwhile, my godmother, who was head of maternity at Worthing Hospital near Brighton, suggested I go there to have my baby, and I was all for it. I arrived there on a Tuesday and they induced me that same day. We were off! My contractions came faster as my labour intensified, and I thought, *My god! I'm going to be leaving this place with this tiny little thing. Nothing will ever be the same.* I gave birth the following day, Wednesday 23 March 2005.

I was well prepared for Tahlia's arrival, and had a great support system around me – everyone excited and ready to meet her. I had everything set up at my house – cot, moses basket, all the baby bits. Once we were home, my family all came round and brought her lots of cute bits and pieces, spoiling us both rotten. After all the fear I'd had about telling my dad, he couldn't wait to meet and look after her when he was back in the country. He even offered to take Tahlia to the Philippines to live with him and my mum while I concentrated on my singing career.

'Thank you, Dad, but my baby is staying with me,' I told him.

Having such a big family around that time was beyond a blessing. I had always helped look after my little sisters when I was younger, and I had played a big part in the lives of my older nieces and nephews. Now it was my turn, and I had plenty of willing arms to help with my child. It was a happy moment in time.

THIRTEEN

IN APRIL 2005, JUST A couple of weeks after Tahlia was born, I was back working again. With our schedule the way it was, there wasn't really any time for the kind of maternity leave a regular nine-to-fiver might have. To be honest, it didn't even cross my mind that that would be an option. My instinct was to just carry on working, and I had no problem with that.

We were still recording *Taller in More Ways* at the time and it had to be finished asap. For this one, we were working with a range of different writers/producers. As well as Xenomania, we worked again with Cameron McVey, who we'd recorded our first album with, and also American producer Dallas Austin, who'd worked with huge artists like TLC, Madonna and Boyz II Men, to name a few. We were often working long hours in the studio, and there were times when we recorded long into the night. Most days, I took Tahlia to the studio with me because I was breastfeeding and thought it was best. Mum and Dad were still away in those early days of motherhood, and my brothers and sisters all had their own stuff going on.

During the sessions, I would be breastfeeding in between vocal takes and then handing Tahlia over to Heidi or Keisha to look after when it was my turn to go in and sing. They both loved having her in the studio and made a huge fuss of her, and to be honest, they were already used to me bringing someone

or something to work with me. Before Tahlia, I would sometimes bring one of my baby nephews into the studio, and if I
didn't have a baby in tow, it might be one of my dogs. I often
had a small child or an animal hanging off me while I worked.

It's not something I would ever think of doing these days,
but back then mayhem followed me!

When I think about juggling early motherhood and intense
studio sessions now, it makes my head spin – even at the time
it was a balance I struggled to find. My nights felt long and
restless. If I wasn't up breastfeeding, I would lie awake at night,
allowing my overactive imagination to run wild – often to an
unhappy or bad place. I was an anxious mum, for sure. The
idea that something might happen to Tahlia or to me was all-
consuming. I'd read about cot-deaths and constantly worried
that something like that would happen to my baby. I'd find
myself standing over her while she slept, putting my fingers
under her nose to make sure she was still breathing. As time
went on, I was in a place that I really shouldn't have been in as
a new mum, catastrophizing about everything: the plane was
going to crash, the world was going to end, this car is going too
fucking fast. Everything was about loss and dying; it was some
weird shit. My mind has always been so demanding of me, so
often leading me down a dark path. It wasn't healthy, but I let
my thoughts get away from me. I think the fact that I now had
this new, tiny little person to take care of brought my darkest fears bubbling to the surface more than ever. *If something
happens to me, who's going to take care of my baby?* I found it
impossible to quieten the noise.

In early October of that year, 2005, we released 'Push The
Button', the first single from our fourth album, and we hit the
number-one spot once again. A couple of weeks later, *Taller in*

More Ways dropped and also went straight to number one in the album charts.

When I watch the video for 'Push The Button' now, I can see how skinny I was. I'd lost so much weight since giving birth that I think it's the slimmest I've ever been. There's a particular photograph of me from around that time where I look like Skeletor from *Masters of the Universe* – my cheekbones are hollow, and I look gaunt. I didn't realize at the time what was happening to me, but I now know that the cocktail of depression, stress, anxiety, plus trying to juggle a crazy work schedule with motherhood, had caught up with me. And now, it was wreaking havoc on my body as well as my mind.

Following 'Push The Button', we released the single 'Ugly' in December. We flew to New York for the video, which was set in an old warehouse, and had various people of all shapes and ages performing audition-like situations while we sang. Tahlia came with me and even had a cameo in the video. The theme of the song is body image and feeling ugly for being different. Ironically, at the time I didn't feel good about myself at all. My head was all over the place, and both mentally and physically, I was drained. Still, there were promotions and performances to do, so for a while I carried on, feeling worse and worse as time went by but not really knowing or understanding why.

Every day felt like a drag. In the morning, I would wake up feeling like I couldn't even face getting out of bed, let alone face the world. I knew I had to because Tahlia needed to be fed and looked after, but I would lie there for a while, looking around my room thinking, *I just can't do it.* Knowing that on top of that, I also had a day of Sugababes work to get through was even more daunting. I didn't realize at the time how bad it had got. While I was living it, I knew it was tough, but I didn't realize the extent to which I was not only struggling, but losing the battle to stay afloat. At the time, I had no idea about postnatal depression. I'm not sure I'd even heard of it, but ultimately, that's what I was suffering with. I desperately needed help.

With my mental health going downhill once again, I ended up seeing various doctors and psychiatrists. My management found places where I could go for help, and I remember trying different ones. A couple of them were in bland, unassuming buildings – one looked like a dentist's from the outside; another was just like an ordinary doctor's surgery with an entrance at the back. It was all kept on the down-low. I don't know if it was to protect me or the group. Maybe my management were keen to keep things private – at the time, I didn't care. I just went wherever the car dropped me. It might sound like I'm being vague about all this, but so much of it is a blur. When I think and write about events around this time, I have to sit and concentrate because so much of it is lost to me. There are whole sections of my memory that I question having happened at all. An event comes into my mind, and I think, *Was that real, or did I make it up?* Sometimes, when I cast my mind back to my Sugababes days and beyond, it feels like one big circle. I can't quite place the order of things. I suppose it's no wonder. There was so much going on in my life – it felt like a blur even then.

On top of everything, I missed my mum and dad terribly while they were away. Sometimes, in my darkest moments, I would call my mum in the middle of the night – her time. Sometimes, I didn't even need her to speak, I just wanted her to stay on the line with me. I was comforted just hearing her breathe. This ended up becoming an obsessive habit. I wasn't meaning to be selfish in worrying Mum, although it really did worry her; I just wasn't thinking straight because I was so down and missing them so much.

They ended up coming home after a few months and I think that was due to my depression. They would have probably preferred the islands to be their for-ever home, but they came back for me. And thank God they did.

In the end, something had to give. I started to feel like I didn't have enough bonding time with my daughter and it was growing harder to keep up with work and being a mum at the same time. Having my daughter so young, at the height of my career, had thrown everything up in the air. I think these days, people are more accepting of women juggling careers with pregnancy and motherhood. Back then, women were often made to feel like they had to do one or the other.

I had to make a choice. I think if I'd had more time after giving birth before I went back to work, things might have been different, but I hadn't had a moment to catch my breath. This was partly because of the demands of the job, the deadlines and the people around me, and partly because I'm so work-driven anyway. I have to do everything a hundred per cent and that gets tiring fast. When Tahlia was born, there had been an album to finish. Everyone was relying on me to step up: the record label, our management. On top of everything, I knew it wasn't just my career I was responsible for: I had Keisha and Heidi to consider. The fear of letting them down weighed heavy, on top of everything else. Still, when our label announced we would be releasing another single from the album, 'Red Dress', I decided things had to change.

The thought of having another video to shoot, another round of promotion, more travel, tipped me over the edge. Enough was enough and I knew I couldn't carry on. The pressure I felt was overwhelming, and the last thing I wanted was to go down the spiral of depression and self-harm again, which is where I might have ended up. So, with my mum's wise words ringing in my ears, 'Never have kids if you can't look after them,' I decided to leave the band. I could have given over Tahlia's care to Mum and Dad more often, and they would have loved that, but that isn't what I wanted. I needed time with my baby. I needed to stop.

It was the hardest decision I'd ever had to make: leaving a group I'd been with since I was twelve or thirteen years old. Now twenty, I could truly say I grew up in that band. It was all I knew. I kept asking myself, *Am I doing the right thing, or am I just doing this because I'm not thinking straight?* My heart was saying, *Don't do it*, but my mind, working overtime, was telling me, *Get out*. Eventually my head won the war. I felt alone and in a dark place. I thought, *Forget everyone, fuck everyone!* Perhaps I should have taken more time to consider what I was giving up, but I was an angry person by then, upset and pissed off with the world. I don't think I even talked it through with the other girls, which of course I should have. I simply told my management what was happening and why, even though I wasn't sure I knew myself.

In December 2005, close to Christmas, I released a statement.

I signed up for being in Sugababes at the age of 13 and have spent my entire life devoted to making and performing music. I think there comes a time when everyone wants to re-evaluate their life and what they want out of it. For me, that time has now come. For a long time, I have been discussing with Heidi and Keisha our plans for the future and it got to the point where I honestly felt that the commitment I would need to make to Sugababes over the next 12 months was something that would become compromised by me.

The management moved very quickly after that, and within a week or so I'd already been replaced. It all seemed so fast, with my vocals on the upcoming single and other songs on the album re-recorded and replaced for a re-released version. Within two weeks they had already released new band photos, and it was as if I'd never been there. Like those years of my life had just been erased. In my darkest moments of doubt, I wondered if Amelle, my replacement, had already been lined up, waiting on the sidelines. The only thing I could do for my sanity was steer clear of everything the Babes were doing. I didn't want to read or see anything about the new line-up, and I didn't want to watch the videos or listen to the new versions of songs that were once part of me. This meant I wasn't in touch with Keisha or Heidi at all, and I felt guilty about that, especially with Keisha. We'd known one another since we were eight; she had always been in my life, and now she wasn't because of a choice I had made. I kept telling myself it was the right thing for me, but for a long time I wished I hadn't left her, given the life we'd lived together. It was too late, though. I'd made my decision, and I so desperately needed time for myself. Now, with Amelle already in the line-up, there really was no going back.

After the dust had settled, I felt scared. I had no idea what I was going to do next, or how I was going to earn money. I'd left school to devote my time to Sugababes, so I didn't even have other skills or qualifications to fall back on. I'd just bought a new house, had a mortgage to pay, and, despite having Jay and

Tahlia with me, felt suddenly adrift. Initially, my depression just got worse. I spent hours at home, full of regret and asking myself, *What the fuck have you just done, Mutya?* I couldn't reverse time and re-join the group. I'd left them at their peak, thinking I was being strong and brave, but now I felt like shit.

FOURTEEN

AFTER A COUPLE OF MONTHS of breathing and living a
normal life, I started to feel better. I took care of my daughter
like a regular mum. This new routine, my new freedom, was a
massive relief and exactly what I had needed. Part of me wished
I'd had that a few months before; wished that things could have
turned out differently. But that's not the way it worked out. As
things were, I felt there was no other option. I tried to push
thoughts of what could have been out of my mind and concentrate on my family.

When Jay, Tahlia and I moved to Hertfordshire, life changed
again. Somehow, I ended up with a Shetland pony, six chick-
ens, two snakes, some cats and eighteen dogs – yes, you read
that right, eighteen. I'd bought the house from a woman who
bred and trained German shepherds for the police force. It had
a massive garden and about seven sets of kennels on a huge
plot of land. Jay and I soon filled up the kennels, and for a
while I became a dog breeder. I wanted a goat too, because
we had so much land, and a hungry goat would have made a
fantastic lawn mower, munching all the grass. Our world was
suddenly hectic and full of life.

For a while, this seemed like the perfect place for us – a
lovely country life. We had quad bikes that we tore around
the land on, and, of course, there was a huge social aspect too.

Friends would come over all the time for gatherings. In fact, I had parties pretty much on a weekly basis, some of them quite extravagant. On Halloween, I'd decorate the entire garden, bringing in smoke machines and all sorts. People would end up staying for two weeks at a time, and we often had my brothers and sisters staying with us too. It was a lively, buzzy existence, very different to the one I have now. I don't think a day went by back then when I didn't have someone round, or a glass in my hand and music playing till stupid hours of the morning. It was a bit like our happy little community back on the estate – animals and all! And no matter how hard we partied, I still always managed to get up and do the school run.

These were happy times together for Jay and me, but eventually things started to turn sour. We were knocking heads over every little thing and my trust in him started to waver. Eventually, we split, but he didn't move far and stayed in Tahlia's life always.

After Jay and I broke up, I wasn't worried for a moment about being on my own. My family were always around me, always supportive, so I never felt like I had no one, and I had no concerns about raising Tahlia as a single mum. She never lacked love or attention because she had me, as well as my family, who adored her and obsessed over her. To me, that was the most incredible and important thing.

I continued breeding dogs, but my music career was still bubbling away in the background, though it took a while after leaving the band before anything started happening. Before I'd left Sugababes, there had been no talk of me having a solo career of my own. When the subject first came up a few weeks after, I resisted. Someone from our label called me and asked if I'd be up for making a solo record and I said no. In truth, I was worried that our fans might think that was the only reason I'd left. The label told me to go away and think about it, and that's what I did.

Eventually, I decided I should go for it. I realized that working on my own record would be different because I'd only have myself to consider. I'd be writing and recording in the studio at my own pace before having to embark on any crazy promo schedules, so I could take things slowly. I'd have to meet new producers and find my sound, and all that would take time. I could set the pace for the first time in my life. I had always loved being in the studio, and had grown pretty confident with creating music myself towards the end, so this could be a really cool moment for me. I also knew that the girls were carrying on with their brand-new member, so me going solo wasn't going to affect them. In the end, I thought, *Why not?* My passion was music and I'd never wanted to quit it for ever. I had to quit the Babes because I needed space and time, but this was a chance for me to return on my own terms.

It wasn't long before I was meeting the new people I would be working with. It was hard, and I didn't particularly enjoy those early days of being a solo artist. I was still trying to get used to the idea that it was just me and that I didn't have two other girls at my side. This wasn't just the case while singing and recording but also in meetings and when it came to making decisions. I'd always had Keisha, Heidi or Siobhan to bounce off, but now the buck stopped with me. My opinion was the only one that mattered.

With my solo album, I knew I wanted people to hear my vocals more. When you're in a girl group with two other voices, everyone has their place. It can sometimes feel quite restrictive, and it's harder to shine through and show people who you are creatively. I feel like everyone saw me as the low, sultry voice of the Sugababes, which wasn't a bad thing by any means, but now I wanted to show what else I could do with my voice. I guess I wanted to surprise people. I was also keen to work on music that I connected with in a more natural way. Over time, the Sugababes sound had become more pop than it had been at the start. Yes, the songs were great and, as pop music goes, it was pretty cool, but I'd grown up listening to and loving R&B, so I wanted to return to those roots with the songs I was recording. I don't think I was looking for a specific sound, I just did what felt right, but that took a lot of work. I went into the studio with a lot of different producers, I travelled to LA to work, and I did several writing camps with various teams of writers to find that perfect fit. Some results were better than others and, naturally, not all the songs made the album. But when a song clicked, I put my all behind it, and kept working on and perfecting it till it was done. I was happy that there was a real mix of genres on the finished product. This wasn't going to end up being a bunch of songs that all sounded the same – each track was different to the previous one, with its own distinct identity.

One of my favourite tracks was 'Suffer For Love', which I wrote with Ali Tennant, Guz Lally, Gus Redmond, Larry Brownlee and Lowrell Simon. It had an R&B feel and vocally was hitting all of those notes I wanted the world to hear. I thoroughly enjoyed my studio sessions with Ali and Guz. 'Wonderful' was written by Redeye, who produced the track with Guy Sigsworth. Redeye were amazing to work with, and that song, for me, was giving Mariah Carey – I loved it. These tunes might not have ended up as singles, but they were songs where I knew I was pushing myself and doing what I wanted to do. I was able to express myself and end up with songs that were authentically Mutya.

In the end, I was very happy with how my album turned out, but, as usual, I didn't let myself acknowledge the achievement or celebrate it. Listening to it recently, I was struck by how young I sound, but also how well it hangs together as an album. And given my situation at the time, I'm so glad I didn't allow myself to go down the tunnel of writing songs of bitterness and hate. So yes, I feel proud to have co-written and recorded *Real Girl*.

As well as all the fantastic songwriters and producers I collaborated with, I had the honour of featuring both George Michael and Amy Winehouse on the album – two incredible artists who are no longer with us. Amy sang vocals on my single 'B Boy Baby', and I duetted with George on 'This Is Not Real Love', which was my first single outside of the band, taken from his greatest hits album *Twenty Five* and remixed for my album.

George had wanted to work with me for a while. In fact, he'd asked to work with me when I was still with the Babes. I wanted to, but the label said no, telling me it wasn't the right time. You can imagine how happy I was about that decision. *Saying no to George Michael – what the fuck?* I'd grown up with George's voice ringing around our house. My mum was a huge Wham! fan and we all loved his solo material. I couldn't believe I was missing out on that chance.

When I left the band, he called me and said, 'I heard you're not with the girls any more, are you still up for doing a duet?'

On the day I was due to go into the studio to record the song, part of me thought it was some sort of prank. Surely I was being punked for a TV show? But then I walked in, and there he was, sitting on a swivel chair at the mixing desk. When he spun around and looked at me, with that familiar smile, I could hardly believe my eyes. I spent most of that day with him, watching him sing and then letting him guide me through my parts. He wanted me to feel free to do my thing in the recording booth, and that felt so good. He was no longer *the* George Michael: he was just this lovely, kind and gentle man. A very cool, beautiful soul.

George had said that he wanted to work with me because I was one of the UK's best singers, and it meant so much to me to hear him say that, let alone repeat those words to the crowds when we sang together on his 25 Live tour in 2006. It was incredible stepping out in front of his audience – something I'll never forget. Before me, George had only recorded with a handful of other women: Aretha Franklin, Mary J. Blige and Whitney Houston. These were all women I'd grown up listening to and admired, so I was in very good company. He was also from the same area of north-west London as me and had gone to my high school for a time, which came as a surprise to both of us and gave us a special connection. One of my favourite things about the experience was helping my mum's dream of meeting George become a reality. She was the one who'd introduced me to his music when I was little, after all. It was quite comical watching them hug. She's so tiny and he was six feet tall, so she just about came up to his waist. But my, she loved meeting her idol, and I felt proud to have been a part of making it happen.

Working with George was a huge boost to my confidence, and really showed me just how freeing being a solo artist could be. I just wish there was more footage of us singing live together. There isn't much, aside from some dodgy 2006 phone camera clips, which, as you can imagine, are not the best!

My collaboration with Amy Winehouse came about because we were both signed to Island Records and had the same artist and repertoire manager, Darcus Beese. I'd known Amy for a while before that; we'd met at various award shows and had a few mutual friends. We always got on well when we saw one another, but never really hung out together. Amy always seemed to have a lot going on in her life, and I had enough craziness going on in my own world. To me, she was a wonderful person and an incredible talent. The song, which uses parts of the Ronettes' classic 'Be My Baby', was produced by Salaam Remi, who originally worked on it with Amy, but they never finished it. When I worked with Salaam, we decided to finish the track, creating 'B Boy Baby' and using Amy's incredible backing vocals on the chorus. For me, it was wonderful to have that connection with her, and even though we didn't record it together, the song is something to treasure. Amy was just two years older than me and, as most people know, struggled with addiction and mental health. I wonder how many of us in the industry were having similar struggles. It makes me sad when I think about how much more she had to give to the world with her music.

Once I let go of all the fear, I had a great time doing my solo album. With all the trauma of leaving the band and upending my life behind me, I was suddenly living again – that was the prevailing mood at the time. My first proper solo single was 'Real Girl', which incorporated a sample of the Lenny Kravitz classic 'It Ain't Over 'Til It's Over'. I was very confident in the choice of single, but I had other concerns around how people might see and perceive the new Mutya Buena. It wasn't just the music I was worried about. Physically, I'd changed a lot too.

As a woman in the public eye, I've always felt a pressure to look a certain way, to be a certain size and body shape. Some shapes and sizes have always been seen as attractive and healthy, while others are seen as bad, unhealthy and ripe for criticism. I often fell into the latter category, and that was hard to hear, especially as a teenager.

In the run-up to releasing 'Real Girl', I did a photo shoot for the *Daily Mail*. It probably wasn't the best move, but at the time, I just saw it as promotion. I remember feeling fairly good about my body and myself when I did the shoot, but when the results appeared in print, I started to find fault in every little thing. It was a throwback to the criticism I'd received while I was in the group, which always seemed to come thick and fast when any new pictures surfaced. If it wasn't about my attitude or moodiness, it was usually targeting weight and body. Whatever form it took, it was always there. I'd felt tortured by it for such a long time that I started to believe that perhaps there was something wrong with my body. Maybe if I could change a few things, I thought, I might feel differently.

I wasn't in the best place at the time, not thinking as clearly as I should have been, which meant I was often focusing on the wrong things. I couldn't seem to be able to sort myself out mentally, so I was concentrating on the things I *could* change. I started obsessing about the physical. I was about to launch as a solo artist. There were no longer three people sharing the spotlight: from now on, all the focus was on me. I wanted people to think, *Wow! Look at how good Mutya looks. She's different now, better!*

With hindsight, I probably shouldn't have done anything at that time. I wasn't in a place to make wise or rational decisions.

After that *Daily Mail* shoot, I first took the plunge – a breast enlargement – which I did at a clinic in London. It was a clinic where several women I knew had gone, but I was nervous.

This was the unknown, and I was worried something would go wrong, as anyone would be. In the end, I went with a friend of mine, and we both had our breasts done at the same time, lying on beds next to one another in recovery. This was the start of a long obsession with trying to change the way I looked.

Whatever people thought about the way I looked, my first solo single went to number two in the UK charts in June 2007, only kept off the number-one slot by 'Umbrella' by Rihanna. 'Real Girl' also went top ten in several other European countries, which meant I got to travel again, but this time it was all for me.

For some reason, they fucking loved me in Russia, so I was there all the time. Poland and Ukraine too – places I'd never touched down in with the Babes. I couldn't believe the reception I got in those countries. I had a fanbase in places I'd never even thought about visiting before. I ended up travelling to Moscow and Kyiv several times, and it was always a vibe. I'd perform at these amazing clubs, parties and events and I was treated like a princess. For the first time in my life, I found myself being whisked through customs to a fleet of waiting cars and security, and looked after like never before. Post-show, I'd always be taken out to the best clubs and restaurants – no expense spared. I had this strange but wonderful glow knowing that *Real Girl* had hit so big in those places. It all felt new and exciting; suddenly I had hope again for a brighter future.

I'll admit, doing promo alone took some getting used to. Being in a band meant I always had a bit of back-up on stage. If I had an off day or my voice wasn't at its best, there was a safety net of sorts, someone to cover my arse. Now, for the first time since performing as a little girl, I was out there on my own. I had to be my own safety net. Every part of the experience was different to what I'd known before, but I quickly got used to it, and even enjoyed it. The upside of flying solo was that I only had myself to worry about. I didn't have to behave in a certain way or cater to anyone else's needs. I could talk about what I wanted to talk about without stepping on somebody's toes. That's not to say I wanted to bad-mouth my past or the Babes. I was always very careful not to speak in a disparaging way about what had gone before in my interviews. That would have been feeding into the negativity that some people were still trying to peddle. My focus was on me and what I was putting out into the world, and I'm proud of myself for that. For the first time, I felt like I had my hand on the wheel. I was in control. It felt weird but nice, and yes, it was empowering.

The second single from my album was 'Song 4 Mutya (Out Of Control)'. This was a collaboration with the British electronic duo Groove Armada. It was originally intended for another singer, Estelle, but after I left Sugababes, the Groove Armada boys decided they wanted to work with me so they approached Island Records to see whether I was interested. They've since said in interviews that they wanted 'an iconic voice' but that they were also quite scared of working with me! They were surprised at how lovely I was in the studio. I guess those misconceptions really hang around!

I recorded the vocals at a house in west London, and the guys were amazing to work with – really cool and laid-back. Before the session, we sat down and discussed how the lyrics would work for me and what I wanted to say.

Those lyrics would eventually cause controversy because the press decided that the song was all about my replacement in Sugababes, Amelle. The line 'That's who has replaced me? / What a diss' was perceived to be aimed at her, which simply wasn't true. The song was about a girl spotting her boyfriend in a car with another girl. Sugababes and Amelle could not have been further from my mind by then; I was having far too much fun recording my own music. Still, I had to defend myself in the press and deny I was sniping at my old bandmates. It's something I still have to set people straight about to this day!

Though our careers were going on separately, and we were all very happy doing our own thing, it felt like other people were really trying to add fuel to the fire. On one occasion, I was invited to an event which Amelle was apparently also going to. On the day of the event, an acquaintance called to tell me that Amelle couldn't wait to see me and to give me a piece of her mind. I was somewhat taken aback – a piece of her mind about what, for fuck's sake? I'd left the band and she had stepped into my shoes – what did she have to be vexed about?

I couldn't even be sure it was true or that she'd actually said it, but because I'd heard similar rumblings before, I was on my guard. Maybe it was just someone trying to stir up shit between us; maybe not. Whatever the ins and outs of it, I was more than ready if she had something to say. I had nothing to be sorry for. As it turned out, Amelle wasn't even at the event in the end, so that was the end of that! There were lots of odd whisperings at that time, and it was hard to tell what was the truth and what was just being blown out of proportion by gossip and the press.

It got worse as my solo career continued. Around that time, I couldn't help but feel like the new line-up of Sugababes didn't even want to be under the same roof as me. That was hurtful because when I left the group, I'd had no problem with her. I didn't know the girl, but when I eventually bumped into her at a recording of *CD:UK* I was friendly and polite. As far as I was concerned at the time, we were all on a new journey with new beginnings. I'd chosen to leave the band, and I was doing my thing, so I had no reason to resent her or have attitude. Still, as I understood it, I made some of them feel uncomfortable, and because of that they didn't want to be at the same events as me. It's hard to know whether people were telling the truth or just stirring shit, but for whatever reason we never seemed to be in the same building. This wouldn't have bothered me, but for the fact that it meant me missing out on certain opportunities to perform. We were both putting out records at the same time, but by then Sugababes were flying. If it came down to a choice between having me or them on a TV show or line-up, I would likely lose the toss. Some things would come my way and then disappear, and eventually I'd see that the girls were doing the gig instead. I don't know where the animosity came from but it was certainly overhyped by the people around us.

It was a weird and horrible time, and often made me feel less-than. It felt like the industry was choosing them over me. I had a young child and a mortgage, and I just wanted to get on and work without feeling overshadowed the whole time.

After that, I started to tell myself that I didn't care; that I didn't give a shit about any of them. I guess it was my way of protecting myself from the pain and sadness of it all. I felt like I'd tried to be the bigger person, but it had been thrown back in my face. In the end, I shut down completely, telling myself that Sugababes meant nothing to me. It was something I regretted for a long time. It meant that I lost my connection with Keisha. Our lives and social circle were so different, it was very unlikely I was ever going to bump into her unless it was in some TV studio and she was with her band. It was all very sad.

Despite all that, 'Song 4 Mutya' kicked arse, reaching number eight on the UK charts and number one on the dance charts.

It also did well in several European countries and Australia and the reviews were fantastic, with the *Guardian* calling it 'the finest pop song since Rihanna's "Umbrella"'!

I performed at some festivals with Groove Armada, and the track was also featured on their album *Soundboy Rock*.

It's only looking back now that I can truly appreciate that song's success. At the time, it sort of passed me by or got lost in everything else that was happening in my life. The bad things, of course, but the exciting things too!

Around that time, 2007, I was asked to open for Prince at the O2 Arena in London, which was a huge deal because I was a massive fan. I could hardly believe it when Phil Griffin, the photographer who shot the *Real Girl* album cover, told me that Prince was actually a big fan of mine too. He even had me as his laptop screensaver. I mean, what the fuck? As far as I was concerned, this was something nobody could take away from me.

On the day of the opening show at the O2, I still couldn't quite believe it was happening. I stood there watching Prince's sound check, having been told by security, 'Don't approach or talk to Prince unless he approaches you.' Those were the rules, and I had no intention of breaking them, at least not with his scary security milling around.

At one point, I could see somebody walking towards me in the auditorium, but the figure was obscured by the light from the stage shining in my eyes. Suddenly, I could make out this small guy in a beanie hat approaching me. It was the man himself. Prince.

'Thanks so much for doing this; I'm a big fan of your music,' he said.

I was taken completely aback. I could've died happy right then, but he went on.

'I'm doing an after-show gig later on. I'd love it if I could sing "Suffer For Love" with you.'

What?

'Suffer For Love' was one of my favourite songs from my album, and here was Prince, asking if he could sing it . . . with me . . . for his guests.

'Yeah, I'll have my band there, so we can just sing together,' he said.

The words 'FUCK YES' shot through my brain, but my joy was short-lived.

Back in my dressing room, my tour manager told me I couldn't go to the after-show gig because we had to leave as soon as the main show was over. I had to be in Sheffield for a TV show very early in the morning, and we'd have to travel overnight to get there on time. I was truly gutted, but there was nothing I could do. To this day, Phil Griffin laughs and tells me, 'I've never known anyone else to turn down the chance to sing with Prince – and singing one of your songs too.'

Unfortunately, the bubble of my solo career didn't last as long as I hoped it would. Despite a MOBO nomination at the end of 2007, in early 2008 I was dropped by Island Records. The reason given was poor sales of my last two singles, 'Just A Little Bit' and 'B Boy Baby', which probably didn't help my case, but I think the truth of it was that I had pissed off someone at the label and that had been escalated. I'd been recording back-to-back interviews for Germany, and I think someone felt I ignored them when they came over. They said I didn't bother to say hello. This wasn't the case – I'd simply been swamped – but I heard from other people at the label that this person wasn't happy with me and they thought I was arrogant. The next thing I knew,

I had been dropped. I've never spoken to the person in question since.

After I left the label, I had a difficult time, even with my management; it was as if everyone had given up on me and I was floating in the ocean, not knowing which way to swim.

It really hit home how out on my own I was when I went to see the movie *Sex and the City 2* with some friends. I'd been knackered that day and typically I fell asleep in the dark comfort of the cinema. At one point during the film, my friends woke me up, excited.

'Mutya, your song is in the movie!'

Sure enough, there it was: 'Real Girl' featured loud and proud in the film. You might think I'd be happy about this, but I had no idea that my biggest single was featured in a huge Hollywood film. Nobody had bothered to tell me. I remember asking myself, had I missed something? I didn't remember anyone telling me. *Did my management not think I'd be excited about this?* I swung between feeling upset and angry and then both at the same time.

When it came to the movie's premiere, I wasn't even invited, while Sugababes performed at the after-party. It felt like a kick in the teeth and I started questioning everything. Despite my success, I started to wonder whether I even wanted to continue in the music business. After a short burst of brightness, I felt like I was falling back into the dark again.

FIFTEEN

AFTER A BRIEF RETURN TO the party circuit when Tahlia was a bit older, I decided to cut down on drinking for a while. I needed to stay away from all that. I'd started to feel depressed and anxious again and the bad times were clearly outweighing the good. I was pleased with myself, knowing it was for the best and that I was making a sensible choice for me, but it was harder than it sounds. At the time, being sober wasn't quite as accepted as it is these days, and the pressure to go out was real. One of my friends didn't like the idea that I was staying home and calming down.

'Just come out anyway, you don't have to drink,' she told me.

'Yeah, I'm not sure I'll be able to do that,' I replied.

It wasn't easy when I knew everyone else there would be knocking back the booze, but I did miss going out. In the end, I thought, *Fuck it! I'll just go and try not to cave.* We ended up at 10 Room, and over the course of the evening my friend got more and more drunk, leaving me on my own at the opposite end of the club. Being sober in an atmosphere like that was grating and dull, and I wasn't sure how long I could keep it up. Turns out, drunk people are really annoying if you haven't had a drink!

Eventually, I went over to look for my friend and found her at a table with a group of people, happily drinking away. I could see she was quite out of it and suggested she should stop drinking and come back to where I was sitting. She wasn't having any of it, so I lingered and kept an eye on her. When she suddenly started snogging one of the girls in front of everyone, I knew she was truly 'mash-up'. I had to get her out of there before things got really out of control. Being stone-cold sober, I could see what a mess she was, and I knew she'd regret what she was doing in view of everyone. I'd been in that sort of situation, but there'd been nobody there to stop me from making a fool of myself. When I pulled her aside and told her we needed to leave, she resisted and told me that the other girl wanted me to 'fuck off!'

'She said what?'

As sober and clear-headed as I was, I saw red. I was furious. I walked over to the girl, and we argued. She starting insulting me, and I'll admit, I lost it and hit her. Within seconds, security was on me, dragging me out of the club. I was thrown out of 10 Room for causing trouble, and the paparazzi were outside waiting with their cameras.

More than anything, I was embarrassed. I hadn't even been drinking. I'd managed to get into a massive row and get thrown out of a bar without a drop of alcohol passing my lips. It was depressing to think this had happened after I was trying so hard to calm down and make better choices. I'd only set out to help my friend, but it had backfired on me big time. I hadn't even wanted to go out that night, and I really regretted not sticking to my guns.

The following morning, a message from a friend said, 'Oh my god, Mutya, you're in the newspapers.'

The story and a shot of me with my arms angrily raised made the *Daily Mail* and it wasn't a flattering picture – they never were. The way they wrote about me was horrible – *angry ex-Sugababe Mutya gets her claws out.* My heart sank when I saw that the *Sun* had printed the story too. My dad bought it religiously. I pictured him walking to the shops, buying his copy, then going back home, sitting down and opening it to a picture of his daughter being thrown out of a club. Not just my dad: what would my mum, my siblings, my aunties and uncles think seeing it? It had been bad thing after bad thing, and I knew how hard it was for my family, having to see all that stuff. I thought I'd turned over a new leaf, but here I was, back to the old mess.

Over the next few days, my head went to all sorts of bad places. I knew certain people would love the fact that I was all over the papers being a big, mad dumbass. I'd given the haters exactly what they wanted. When I started thinking like that, I couldn't stop. I went to sleep and dreamed about it and would wake up kicking myself. It was a dark spiral I knew too well.

After the incident at the club making the papers, it felt like my attempt at changing my life and going sober had failed. I think that was when my depression really started to kick in. It felt like no matter what I did to try to be better, I was doomed to fail. I was moody, angry, drunk Mutya, and people were never going to accept me as anything else.

It was around this time that I started doing reality TV for the first time. It had been a year since my record label dropped me and I wanted to keep my foot in the door; I was scared of being forgotten, scared of being left behind in such a fast-moving industry. Plus, I had a bloody mortgage to pay! I was hesitant at first, but I finally gave in and agreed to do *Celebrity Big Brother.* The show's producers had been after me for a while. This time around, I thought I should at least give it a try. If nothing else, maybe this would be the thing that allowed people to see a different side of me.

At the time, I was still living in the same house filled with animals, being a full-time mum to Tahlia, and breeding dogs on the side. Music-wise, I was blessed to have the love and support of the LGBTQ+ community, who were always there for me, despite the sudden halt in my career. All through that difficult period, I was being booked to do shows at LGBTQ+ clubs and events – places like the Vauxhall Tavern, Heaven and the Two Brewers in Clapham – I will always have such love for that community. They were the people who still wanted me after I'd been dropped by the label, and still do, to this day. Their support has been unwavering. Those occasional shows kept me singing, but weren't quite enough to keep me going financially.

With *Big Brother*, I wasn't wholly into the idea of exposing myself on national TV that way, especially when so much of it was live, but the money was good, and it was only a few weeks. I thought, *What's the worst that can happen?!* Looking back, though, I wish I'd listened to my gut because I cringe whenever I think about that show now. But you can't change the past.

The good news was that I was in the Big Brother House with some really cool people. La Toya Jackson was very quiet but lovely. Coolio was a character and quite controversial, but I really liked him, and Verne Troyer, who played Mini-Me in the *Austin Powers* movies, was bloody hilarious. One particularly memorable night, he had a little too much beer and decided to drive straight at the diary-room door on his scooter. With dark glasses on, he deliberately zoomed bang into the closed door and got reprimanded by Big Brother for putting his safety at risk. There was always something silly going on in that house!

Both he and Coolio have since sadly passed away. I'm very

honoured to have been able to spend time in such close contact with them, even if it was absolutely bonkers!

Also in the house was Michelle Heaton from Liberty X, who I already knew well, and actress Tina Malone from the TV show *Shameless*, who I absolutely adored. In fact, she was basically like a mum to me while I was in there.

Despite the good company, though, being in the house really messed with my head. You were woken up whenever they felt like waking you up, and there were several clocks dotted around, which all said different times. The whole set-up was created to make sure we lost all sense of reality, and while it makes good telly, it meant that we were constantly on edge.

There was an occasion when we made a big shopping list, only to have it replaced with a measly lunchbox each. Other times we had no hot water unless we won a task. Of course, it was all part of the game, but I found it hard going.

One of my tasks, along with presenter Terry Christian, was rushing out into the garden to worship a statue every time Chesney Hawkes' 'The One And Only' was played. The song might boom out of the speakers in the house any time of the day or night, and we had to get up and worship. We failed this task miserably!

On another day, La Toya and I learned a song that we played on a giant keyboard, jumping from one key to another. For this, I was dressed as a fucking clown doll – big red nose, big red cheeks. Embarrassing doesn't even cover it, and by that point, I was kind of over the idea of making myself look like an idiot in front of the viewing public. Don't get me wrong, I can look back now and accept it as a life experience. If I'm in a good mood I can even laugh at the memories, but it's not something I'd ever do again. Lord Jesus, no!

As the days went on, I turned into a chain-smoker. When you're sitting around as much as we were and unable to go out, smoking felt like the only pastime we had. Meanwhile, my dad, who didn't even know I smoked, was watching on the sofa with my mum and was shocked to see his little girl puffing like a chimney in the Big Brother garden.

'My, Mutya smokes a lot!'

To be honest, I'd almost forgotten that my family were tuning in and watching me the whole time. I hadn't even thought that my dad would catch me smoking like a naughty schoolgirl!

On top of the degrading challenges and the claustrophobia, it was so hard being away from Tahlia for such an extended period. She was four years old at the time, and knowing that she wasn't even that far away made it even worse (I lived quite close to Elstree Studios, where *Celebrity Big Brother* was filmed). Some days I cried my eyes out because I missed her so much. At one point the contestants received messages from loved ones on the outside, and the sight of her smiling and sending me love via video destroyed me. One minute I was sobbing like a crazy mess, and the next I was thinking, *For fuck's sake, the sight of me bawling is going out on the nation's TV screens!* The funny thing was, the reaction to my tears was mostly a positive one. So many people later told me how much they loved seeing that I had a soft, vulnerable side to me. I wondered how they'd seen me before that – like some kind of emotionless robot, perhaps? I wasn't sure whether to take it as a compliment or be offended. It was another reminder that people had no idea who I really was.

One morning, my skin started to flare up quite badly. I have very sensitive skin and have to be careful what I put on it. Feeling irritated and itchy, I went to the diary room to ask to see a dermatologist or a doctor. I had been promised before I entered the house that any medical issues would be taken care of straight away, but I didn't feel like I was taken seriously and I wasn't able to see a doctor as quickly as I would have liked. By the time I finally got some medical attention, I was so embarrassed about being on live TV looking the way I did, with a rash and a swollen face, that I wore a bandana around my face, which looked ridiculous.

That was the beginning of the end for me, and it was compounded by the fact that I missed Tahlia so terribly.

On the second week, I was up for eviction along with three others, but when Tina was evicted instead of me, I decided I had to go too.

There was no big, dramatic storming-out; it was all very calm and considered. I simply told the production team I wanted to leave and they arranged it. I couldn't see myself lasting another week there, making a fool of myself and missing my daughter as much as I did. I would never judge anyone else for doing *Celebrity Big Brother*, but it just wasn't for me. It was one of those TV experiences where you can't help but expose your fears and vulnerabilities. The cameras catch you crying, not looking your best, and sometimes not behaving in the way you normally would because the environment you've been put in is so unnatural. It can bring out a side of you that you'd prefer the world not see.

Once I was out, I discovered that I was one of the favourites to win, according to Ladbrokes, which made me smile.

One thing I'm happy about is that there wasn't as much social media around when I did *Big Brother*. There was Facebook and Twitter, but both were quite young and hadn't blown up in the way social media has now. I'm not sure how I would have dealt with the online criticism and negativity that comes with all that.

Since my reality TV debut, I've done quite a few TV shows and most recently had a great time appearing on *MasterChef*. It helped that I enjoy cooking, but even with that, I worried that I might attract criticism. It's one thing for people to have a go at my looks or my singing – but criticize my cooking? Well, that's just not cool!

I've grown to enjoy doing these kinds of shows much more now, but I still can't quite shake the anxiety that follows it. It's a strange thing. While I was in the *MasterChef* kitchen, I thoroughly enjoyed myself, but when I think about it now, there are things that make me cringe. It's just the way my overactive mind works, I suppose. I worry that people are going to say mean things or that something I've done is going to end up posted on someone's Instagram page as a joke. With social media, it feels like no silly thing you do goes unnoticed. Before, it would be embarrassing when the show aired, and maybe for a few more days if the press picked up on it, but then it was pretty much forgotten. There was no posting on Instagram with a bunch of other people adding their comments underneath – good and bad. Nowadays, everything lasts for ever on the internet, and a cringey few seconds becomes a meme that lives on. I'm so glad it wasn't around in the early days of the Babes – but perhaps it'll move back in the other direction.

I read recently that TikTok is fighting a ban in the US, and in Australia they are soon imposing the world's strictest age laws regarding social media, with no one under sixteen allowed to use it. It's the highest minimum age set by any country, and doesn't even exclude kids who have parental consent. I have mixed feelings about it because I do believe that people need to step away from screens and go out into the world. I've noticed so many people – young and old – who spend their lives with their noses in their phones, forgetting there's a real world out there to enjoy. Perhaps some young people do need more guidance to stop it becoming a lifetime habit.

All that said, there are some positive aspects to social media, especially if you're a creative or musician putting your work out into the world. Those big social platforms are a brilliant way to reach people and communities you might have once struggled to reach. Back in the day, communication with our fans was limited to our shows, or them turning up if we did a personal appearance or a record-signing at HMV. Now, the world has opened up for all of us.

Even the way we meet people and form relationships has changed massively in the last few years, with a million dating apps and ways of connecting.

In 2018, I appeared on *Celebs Go Dating*, and again, that was another tricky experience. The thing about any reality TV show is that, in the end, the most important thing is always the show itself, never the people in it. It's the content and enter-tainment factor that matters. While I was on the show, I felt like I had to behave in a certain way to create the most drama, but hey, I guess that's the way it is with these shows.

The idea is that with each series, a group of celebrities go on a journey to find romance via a celebrity dating agency that pairs them with hand-picked members of the public. I'd never been a great dater and I'd been single for a while, so I thought this might be a good opportunity to test myself. This was something I wouldn't normally do, and we all have to push ourselves out of that comfort zone sometimes, don't we?

The locations for dates can be any venue where they are happy to allow filming, and you're expected to go out on quite a few dates in a short space of time. As well as that, there are the organized 'mixers', where the celebs mix with big groups of potential love-mates in a large social setting.

While you're at the mixers, the drinks are free and flowing, which, given my track record, is probably not the best idea in the world. Believe it or not, I'm quite socially awkward, so a bit of Dutch courage felt necessary if I was going to be able to walk up to perfect strangers and start getting to know them. I'm more confident if the person is a quiet soul, but if someone is forward or overly loud, I tend to draw back a bit. As you can imagine, the type of contestants they have on shows like this are not generally shy, so I knew I would need something to get my engine going.

My first mixer was horribly embarrassing. It started OK, with me at the bar, chatting away with various people and doing shots, not really thinking about homing in on any particular person. There was a guy I got talking to, Jordan, who I felt I got along with. But by the time we got into our conversation, I was pretty drunk – I think I was probably chewing his ear off about all sorts of shit. When we came to the section of the show where the celebs have to choose a person to go on a date with, I didn't feel like I'd especially connected with anyone – certainly not enough to date them anyway.

'Can I choose nobody?' I asked, but the producers told me I had to pick one from the people I'd met.

'Really? But I'm not sure,' I said.

In the end, I felt I had to go with Jordan because we'd been talking for a while. He seemed like a nice guy, but I wasn't sure he was my type. Still, I felt I had to do it and, influenced by the alcohol flowing through my system, I did. I lined up with all the other celebs, facing a room full of 'non-celebs', and I chose Jordan. Then the presenters asked him if he would accept my offer.

'I'm honoured,' he replied, 'but I think we connected on a friendship level, so no, I don't accept.'

Fucking hell!

It was mortifying that he'd said no, especially as I'd only chosen him because I was encouraged to. And on TV no less! But then, magazine editor and *The Only Way is Essex* star Vas Morgan stuck up for me, bringing even more unwanted atten-tion my way.

'How dare you do that?' he said to poor Jordan. 'Do you know who she is?'

Vas is someone I really like, and it was sweet of him to stand up for me, but by then, I just wanted the floor to open and swallow me up.

Meanwhile, while I was begging Vas not to make it any worse than it was already, Chloe Simms, also from *TOWIE*, jumped in and had a go. Jesus Christ, the last thing I needed was even more embarrassment piled on. The whole episode made me feel like I'd been set up.

Some of the contestants up for dating are real characters. One guy I went on a date with spent the whole time talking about the fact that he went to the gym. He must have said the word 'gym' about fifty times in the first ten minutes of our date. This most definitely wasn't the guy for me, so I made my excuses and left.

One of the other issues about the show was how much I ate and drank. Everything was free, so, of course, I just went for it. When you're filming a date four or five times each week for a couple of weeks, it takes its toll on your waistline, let me tell you. In the end, I did have some fun doing the show, and it's quite comical to look back on. At least I can laugh about it now.

Of all the TV shows I've done, *Celebrity Coach Trip*, which I won along with my partner on the show, Lisa Maffia, was a favourite. The idea is that you go on a coach trip around Europe with other pairs of celebs, and vote each other out depending on how much of a team-player you are and how you gelled with the rest of the group. God knows how we won because there were quite a few bits I didn't participate in. The coach trip was from Barcelona to Benidorm, and many of the challenges involved water – paddleboarding, kayaking and water zorbing. I did some of them, but not being the world's best swimmer I ducked out of others. Flyboarding, where you hover above the sea with water jets shooting out of nozzles. For fuck's sake, no! Sorry, I just wasn't ready to die on TV. I was more at home looking pretty and tanning in the sun – that I could do! The body-painting and paella-making were OK by me too!

Lisa and I giggled our way through the experience, trying not to be too competitive but at the same time really wanting to win. Between us, we'd be plotting and planning what we should do one minute, and not really caring the next. I think it was our personalities rather than our skill during the tasks that won us the crown in the end.

It was especially fun meeting some of the other celeb passengers on the coach: Jedward, Big Narstie and Stevo the Madman, and the show's host, Brendan Sheerin, who is just lovely. It was only ever going to be hilarious, but with such big personalities there were a few clashes and fights along the way too. But hey, it's reality TV, after all! I'd certainly do that one again.

My attitude with all this is, if it feels good, do it. I don't want to limit myself in the entertainment industry. First and foremost, I'm a singer and songwriter, but if the right vehicle comes along, there's nothing wrong with a bit of reality telly.

Of course, I've been asked a few times to appear as a contestant on the big shows, like *Strictly Come Dancing*, and there are always plenty of other things in the pipeline, but it's always best to choose them wisely. There are pros and cons to any of these shows and I love watching them, but that doesn't necessarily mean it's a good idea to be on them. Have I learned my lesson from some of my earlier TV experiences? I guess we'll have to wait and see!

SIXTEEN

AFTER MY SOLO DEAL ENDED, I felt like I was out on my own, and I often found myself wondering what I would do next. My mind kept returning to how I had to pull out of school early and all the things I missed out on because of that. To compensate for giving up my education, I've always been very drawn to learning new things as an adult. My sister Dalisay never forgets anything, and she recently reminded me about some of the random interests I've had over the years. I was always trying to improve myself and broaden my horizons after my music career slowed down.

Child psychology was something that I became very interested in – looking into how young people's minds work and why kids act and behave in certain ways. I've always been very engaged with the issue and think a lot about the welfare of children. Maybe it's because I came from a big family with so many different personalities at play under the same roof. Or maybe it stems from how we were looked after, or not, as children in the music industry.

If I see a child who looks sad or in despair, I feel emotional. I often wonder what they are going through, and those thoughts stay with me. That was what made me start researching into what I could do that aligned with that interest. I found a university app where I could look up various classes and courses and applied to take an online Introduction to Child Psychology course. I never thought of it as a new career path, but I thoroughly enjoyed doing it.

As my joy of learning new things grew, it became sort of addictive. It's important to me to keep the brain ticking all the time, particularly as a lot of my work comes easy to me; it's all instinct rather than intellectually challenging. Yes, it can be hard graft, but walking out on a stage and singing is something that comes very naturally to me. The rest, doing TV or press interviews, etc., is a mix of common sense and personality.

So yes, learning and soaking up new things became a bit of a thing for me after my record deal ended.

About a month after starting that course, I thought I'd try something else, something more practical on top of that. I'd always wanted to learn how to do nails properly. If you know me, you know I love to look good, but sometimes I prefer to be able to do these things for myself. So, while I was in the middle of the child psychology course, I also did manicurist and nail technician training. On top of that, I also piled on a hairdressing course, and if there was any spare time in between all that, you'd probably find me at home painting, which I still loved doing as much as I had when I was a child. At one point, spurred on by my love of tattoos, I even spent two weeks observing at a tattoo parlour.

Even now, as busy as I am, I still hold that longing to master new things. One of the things I've always wanted to learn – and people sometimes find this odd or morbid – is embalming. I don't know where the hell that came from, and I think it's a two- to three-year apprenticeship, so it's probably not happening any time soon, but I was always interested in the idea of caring for people after they have passed. Don't be surprised if I open a funeral home one day.

All this was just me making up for lost time, satisfying my craving to learn. The habit was good for me, and the more I learned, the more I enjoyed it. In some ways, it made up for the fact that I missed out on so much. Not entirely, though. You can't go back in time. I still have regrets about not going to college or university. I recently went to my nephew's graduation, and while I felt incredibly proud watching him, a small part of me felt sad. I asked myself, *Why didn't I do this?* As much as I'm a successful, grown-arse woman now, there is still a child inside that sometimes feels unfulfilled. It's like something is missing or there's a part of me I haven't satisfied yet. There's still so much more I want to do.

Still, I'm glad of the skills I've been able to pick up as an adult. As well as the kick I got from learning new things, I could always hear my dad's voice reminding me that it's always good to have something to fall back on. And he's right, you never know. I've been lucky enough to have had an amazing career over so many years, but there was always the chance that things could end. I had to be able to pick myself up and think of a plan B.

That's not to say there weren't still new opportunities for me as an artist, and I had no intention of giving up on the music industry. I was heading towards the second half of my twenties with a five-year-old child, but I still had great friends in the industry and there were often opportunities coming my way.

In September 2010, I was asked to sing on an album called *The Sound of Camden*. The album was to be recorded in Israel with producer Roy Sela, who I was introduced to by one of the owners of Camden restaurant/bar Gilgamesh. It was going to be a collection of quirky cover versions of songs by artists like Radiohead, U2 and Nirvana.

I loved making the record because it allowed me to spread my wings and do something different. I enjoy so many different styles of music, so being able to do something left-field, something with a more indie vibe, felt good. I covered songs like 'Sunday Bloody Sunday' by U2, Radiohead's 'Creep' and Nirvana's 'Come As You Are'. I loved these songs and had grown up listening to them, but I would never have dreamed of covering them.

Around that time, I also recorded and released a track called 'Be OK' with City Boy Soul, a band consisting of Coree Richards of Damage, and rapper Gak Jonze, and I also sung lead vocals on a dance track called 'Give Me Love' for DJ/ producer Paul Morrell. These were much more low-key releases than I was used to, but it also meant there was less pressure that came with them. I didn't have plans to release any more solo music, but along with the courses, some gigs and being a mum, at least I was ticking over.

When I look back on that time between 2009 and 2012, it feels like I was juggling a whole lot of stuff, trying to keep too many balls in the air at the same time. I had a lot more time on my hands than I was used to. I constantly felt like I should be doing something, and I certainly wasn't going to sit at home waiting for life to happen. I had to go out there and find it.

SEVENTEEN

THE OTHER DAY, SIOBHAN AND I were talking about domestic abuse and some of the scary and unbelievable statistics we'd seen on the subject.

Fact: The police receive a domestic-abuse-related call every 30 seconds.

Fact: 1 in 4 women in England and Wales will experience domestic abuse in her lifetime.

Fact: On average, one woman is killed by an abusive partner or ex every five days in England and Wales.

Fact: 93% of defendants in domestic abuse cases are male; 84% of victims are female. And yet, women are three times more likely to be arrested for incidents of abuse.

These are all facts taken from the website of Refuge, an organization for women and children affected by domestic violence.

It amazes and upsets me to think about how many are suffering at the hands of people they're in a relationship with, and no, not all of those are women – but most are.

For me, it's important to touch down and talk about this issue because it has affected me in the past, even though I haven't really talked about it before. It's very easy to look at pop stars and celebrities and think they're leading these amazing, wonderful lives but, of course, it's not always the case.

I had two partners back-to-back who were, in many ways, very similar. Let's call the first one Pauly, though that's not his real name. I met him online, believe it or not! He was a plumber but we seemed quite similar and had the same interests, and ended up really hitting it off! We started chatting back and forth until we eventually exchanged phone numbers and started talking properly.

On our first date, he seemed legit, the real deal, and I liked him a lot. He was good-looking, and we were close in age. After several meet-ups, I felt we were a good fit and over time the good fit turned into a full-on relationship.

Eventually, Pauly moved into my place. It was one of those situations where there wasn't a big discussion, it just gradually happened. One where I didn't really know he was moving in until he was already there. I'd probably seen the warning signs by then, but I was still getting to know him and blinded by my feelings, which were pretty strong. I had messages from friends asking, 'What are you doing?' worried that I was moving too fast, but I ignored them. I felt like I'd had too many people giving me opinions on how to live my life and I didn't want to hear any more. By the time I realized my mistake, I was already caught up in the motion of it all. I felt like there was no going back.

Not long after he moved in, the problems started, and as time went on, more and more stuff came to light. His car was not actually his car; his flat wasn't his flat. Almost nothing he'd told me about himself was true.

Sometimes, he would take my car keys and disappear with my car for days, not calling or considering me at all. When I confronted him about it, we'd always get into a fight. We fought about many things, and the longer it went on, the worse the battles got. He drank a lot, but then so did I. As time went on, he became abusive, both mentally and physically. Then he started following me, turning up at places he didn't need to be. I felt like I couldn't get away from him.

People who knew us continued to say, 'Oh my god, you're with Pauly? Why?'

A few of them thought he was bad news and that he had a screw loose, but I was at a point where I didn't know how to answer and I couldn't see what they saw anyway. There were moments during our relationship when I clearly wasn't in my right mind, behaving in ways I normally wouldn't have, and accepting situations I really shouldn't have.

One night, we were mid-argument while I sat with Tahlia between my legs doing her hair. Suddenly, he leaped up, jumping right over her to attack me, punching and kicking while she was right there beneath us. It wasn't the only time something like that happened, and much of it was alcohol-fuelled.

It's not like I didn't fight back; I did. However low I felt, the idea of a man putting his hand on me, on any woman, was unacceptable, and I did all I could to stop it. Sometimes, though, I just wasn't strong enough. Of course, more than anything I was worried about what Tahlia was seeing, hearing and feeling, but I wasn't present enough to step away or take charge of my situation. I still gave Tahlia my all and looked after her, but my mind was all over the place.

On one occasion, I had to call my sister to come down and step in because I felt like things were seriously out of control. Pauly had attacked me, and I was pretty sure there was more to come. She arrived with a baseball bat, so if he came at me again, she would be ready for him.

I knew the sensible thing would be to tell the rest of my family what was happening, but I was scared. I felt embarrassed telling my parents about the situation I'd got myself into and worried that if my brothers found out, they might take matters into their own hands. That was the last thing I wanted: my brothers getting into trouble on my account. I also didn't want Pauly to be harmed in any way or even arrested, despite what he was doing to me. I guess that's the messy thing about it all. Someone can cause you mental and physical harm and yet you can still love them. Pauly knew how I felt about involving my family, and he used that to his advantage. As far as he was concerned, he could do whatever he wanted, knowing I wouldn't go asking anyone for help.

I tried to get him to leave, but he wouldn't. In the end, my life became too miserable to stay. Pauly was abusive and owed me money, and after months of trying to hide what was going on, I'd become isolated. Eventually, I took Tahlia, left my own house and moved in with my mum. But even then, I played down the situation to my parents. They knew things were bad between Pauly and me, but I was too ashamed to admit that I'd let myself be treated like that, and couldn't face the idea of saying it out loud to them.

I figured Pauly wouldn't want to stay at my house if I wasn't there, and that might be the best way to get rid of him. To speed up the process, I turned off the electricity and even stopped paying all the bills, hoping everything would get cut off. It got so cold in the house at one point, you could see your breath inside, but still, he just wouldn't budge. On one occasion, when he left the premises, I managed to get in and shut him out, but he just climbed through a window while I was out.

Meanwhile, I was living at my mum's and he would come and sit outside her house for hours or lurk around corners, waiting for me. Whenever I went to leave the house, I could feel his presence and eyes on me, and out and about, there was always a shadowy figure in a hoodie lurking not far behind.

One day, when I needed to go out, I could see Pauly in a car across the road. He was wearing his hoodie as usual and sitting low in the seat, but I knew it was him. In the end, I bit the bullet and called Tahlia's dad, Jay. I still didn't want to involve my brothers, so he was the only one I felt I could turn to.

'I feel embarrassed calling you,' I told him. 'It's the last thing I wanted to do, but I need your help.'

By the time Jay got there, Pauly had been sitting there for over an hour. Jay walked over to the car and pulled the door open.

'What are you doing here?' he said.

Pauly told Jay that he was only there to give me back the money he owed me.

'Well, give it to me, and I'll give it to her,' Jay said. 'You don't need to see Mutya. You don't need to have any contact with her.'

Pauly demanded to see me face-to-face, but that didn't go down well with Jay, who refused to let him see me. It probably won't surprise you to learn that there was no money.

'So why are you here waiting for her?' Jay asked again. 'What's the real reason?'

With that, Pauly reversed the car and sped away, but Jay followed him, just to make sure he left the area.

I was grateful, of course, but my relief didn't last long. Pauly did this repeatedly; I just couldn't get rid of him. I'd never felt so trapped.

On one occasion, he turned up outside my friend's house while I was there, and on another, he chased me in his car.

It's unbelievably scary being chased by someone who wants to do you harm. I felt sick to my stomach. I'd left him, but still couldn't shake him.

One day, he called me from my house yelling, 'There's police here, there's police outside your house.' I had security cameras at the house, so that was a lie that was very easy to uncover. I couldn't work out what he was trying to achieve, but he just wouldn't stop. Even when I called the police and reported his behaviour, it went on.

Eventually, living in my house with no utilities started to take its toll on Pauly. One day, I went to check out the house with some friends to find he'd finally given up and moved out. At last, I could reclaim my home.

I hadn't seen the last of him, however. A few months later, back in the real world and living my life again, I started hosting a live mic night with one of my good friends at a nice little venue in Kilburn. It was a weekly gig where local artists could get up and perform their material, and it gave me something fun to focus on. It was always a good night out and I loved hosting it.

One week, I was buzzing around the venue when I heard a voice I knew all too well singing on the mic. My blood ran cold, and I looked up towards the stage. It was Pauly. This was no coincidence; he knew full well it was my night. It was billed as Mutya Buena's open-mic night, so he'd deliberately turned up to intimidate me.

That familiar fear was back immediately, even though I was surrounded by friends who would never have let anything bad happen. It felt like however hard I tried to get my freedom back, nothing had changed. Once I'd got my head around what was going on, I rushed over to the friend I ran the night with.

'What the fuck is he doing here?' I shouted.

She told me Pauly had turned up with some friends and spoken with her.

'He told me he'd asked you if he could sing, and you'd agreed.'

'Well, he's lying as usual,' I said. 'I had no idea he was here until I heard his voice.'

I probably could have handled things better, but I was in panic mode by then.

I started screaming, 'Get him off the mic, get him out!'

The band stopped playing while everyone looked at one another, wondering what the hell was happening. After that, he was escorted off the stage and told to leave.

That wasn't the end of it, though. Of course it wasn't. Once he was out of the venue, he stood outside, demanding to talk to me. By then, I'd had time for everything he'd ever done to sink in, so there was no way I was going out there. Some of my male friends went outside and told him I wasn't going to talk to him and to 'fuck off'. But as we know from the weeks he refused to leave my freezing house, he's a relentless guy, so it took a while for him to give in and move.

The fact that he'd turned up at my night and lied to my friend, knowing his presence would upset and unnerve me, spoke to me about how manipulative he was and always had been. Looking at him that night had been an eye-opening experience – like seeing him in a completely different light. This person that I'd once been attracted to now looked ugly to me, and I couldn't work out what I'd ever seen in him or what I'd been doing with him in the first place.

Mercifully, I haven't seen him again since that night.

There are so many things I would have done differently now. I wish I'd let my family know what was happening; I wish

I'd been tougher in getting him out of my house. Hindsight doesn't help, though. I simply didn't have the strength then that I do now.

The lesson here is that we need other people. Most of us have someone we can trust who would be willing to help in a situation like the one I found myself in. I was so embarrassed about what was going on that I couldn't even speak to my best friend. Don't do that! My advice to women in this predicament is to pick up the phone if you can. Tell a friend, tell a family member, or find a charity or organization that can support you. Don't let embarrassment, shame and fear rule you. You deserve better.

EIGHTEEN

THROUGHOUT THE YEARS, SIOBHAN AND I had stayed in touch, but not in any major way. We saw each other from time to time, bumping into one another at the odd social event, and it was always nice to catch up. As far as Keisha went, I still remembered her as a beautiful, supportive friend and big sister, despite us not being in one another's lives. I missed her (we've since spoken about it, and she felt the same). In fact, when I sat down and thought about our long separation from one another, I realized that it was having to watch the band move on without me that had hurt. I had no hard feelings towards Keisha.

When I first heard Keisha was leaving the Babes back in 2009, Siobhan and I discussed the idea of us all getting together again, though it felt like a long shot. We eventually reached out to Keisha through a lawyer, about nine months later, but she resisted. Keisha later said in an interview that she was hesitant because she needed to heal. She felt 'girl-banded' out, which of course I could relate to. It took a while before she was ready to think about it seriously. In fact, it wasn't until 2011 that things really started to move.

But before anything could happen, there were a few things that needed to be resolved; things from the past that needed to be laid to rest. It had been ten years since the original three parted company. I know, ten! Since then, so much had happened. We weren't kids any more. It wasn't as simple as just getting back together. We'd have to get to know one another all over again and learn about the women each of us had become.

We met up just to see how we got along. Keisha and Siobhan went out a couple of times because it had been such a long time since they'd sat down together and talked. After that, the three of us went for dinner to move things forward, but it was a while before anything concrete happened. It felt good being together. For me, there was unfinished business between Siobhan, Keisha and me. We'd had something fantastic as kids, something magical, but we hadn't reached our full potential. Firstly, we were all too young to appreciate and nurture our talent, and secondly, we never had enough time together as a trio to show the world what we could do.

In some ways, it was hard for me to get my head around. I'd spent so long as a solo performer that it wasn't going to be easy for me to jump back into a group situation. I was looking at these two girls I'd grown up with, now adults, and with a lot of water under the bridge. I'd missed them, but I had loved the freedom of recording and performing on my own. Could I go back to the responsibility of being part of a whole? I hadn't forgotten how that ended the last time. On top of that, my life was shaky. Things weren't easy for me. This was while I was still in a relationship with Pauly, and I was using drugs and drinking. For a while, I'd been existing rather than living, and I wasn't sure if I was in a place where other people could rely on me. I couldn't help but think about how it had been before, when I was the so-called wild child of the band. How would I feel knowing that Siobhan and Keisha had moved on and grown up while, in some ways, I was walking the same path? It was a while before I would let the girls in on some of the things I'd gone through. Right then, I wanted to keep it all about positivity and moving forward. But the worries still lingered.

Once we'd sorted out the logistics, we decided it was time to make some music. It felt natural and right when we finally got back into a studio together. We were finishing what we started. We'd only recorded one album together as a trio, and this was our chance to turn back time and see where that might have led if things had been different. I told *Billboard* magazine in an interview, 'Our lives, I don't think, would have been complete if we didn't do this,' and I meant it!

In April 2012, we signed with Polydor Records, and a couple of months later, we confirmed that we'd reformed under the name Mutya Keisha Siobhan, or MKS for short. It didn't feel right coming up with some brand-new band name. We were the OG Sugababes, and if we couldn't legally have that name, why not just use the names everyone knew us by. Our first public appearance together was at the 2012 Olympic Games opening ceremony in London. We weren't performing, but everyone saw us there together. It was our first appearance together in eleven years and we posted it on Instagram. After that, it all suddenly felt real. The most recent iteration of Sugababes had gone on hiatus and the fans started buzzing about the idea of the original line-up together again. They hadn't seen our faces together for so long, and they wanted to know what was happening next.

The trouble was that it was studio time at work and struggle time at home. At this point, my relationship with Pauly had gone from bad to worse, and I wasn't in control of my drinking. Not wanting to worry the other girls, I was lying to them and myself about how lost I was. We weren't kids any more: we were all grown up and had our own lives. Unfortunately, I felt like mine was the shittiest one, and I found that hard to accept. Consequently, I was pretending my life was something better than it was to cover up my embarrassment over the truth. It was a struggle to keep up the pretence.

During 2012, while we were recording, I was in a very dark place. Mentally, I was not myself at all. I'd tried pulling myself together, to find the energy to get out there and work, but the depression I was suffering was stronger than any will I had, and it just kept pulling me back under. What was so shocking about it was the force at which it hit me, seemingly from nowhere. Yes, I'd had depression when I was younger, and for a period when I'd first had my daughter, but since then I'd gone through better, brighter times. Perhaps I thought I'd beaten it, I don't know, but here it was again, stronger and meaner than ever. It didn't help that I was drinking and self-medicating to try to ease the pain. Nothing I did could pull me out of it.

It's not like I didn't have support around me. My family and friends were constantly reminding me that they were there, and Keisha and Siobhan were amazing and supportive throughout too.

At the time, we had work scheduled and studio time booked; we were really trying to make MKS work. But I was nowhere to be found half the time, not answering phone calls or turning up to places I was supposed to be – all the usual hallmarks of a depressed person and a throwback to the days where I would disappear on a bender. But this time I wasn't bouncing from party to party: I was hiding from the world.

The trouble was, this had become the norm for me, to the point where I didn't even know how bad it had become. At the start of it all, if you'd have told me I was depressed I would have laughed in your face. I was happy sleeping all day and not facing life. I was totally oblivious to the fact that I was miserable and aggressive towards the people around me, and when I was drinking and doing other stuff, I would have even sworn I was having a good time. I told myself the Xanax and sleeping tablets I was popping were necessary to keep me grounded and help me sleep. It had got to a point where I would go to sleep and wake up days later.

As time went on, I started to get paranoid, feeling like everyone was against me. I hid from people, drinking and doing whatever else I felt like at home on my own. I always did my absolute best to be a good mum to Tahlia, but if ever there was a time when I needed help with that, it was then. Thankfully, in addition to my supportive family, Jay was on hand to take care of her. To be a capable, loving, present parent, you have to be well yourself, and I clearly wasn't. I was aware enough to know that, and Tahlia's welfare was never something I took lightly. If I wasn't feeling my best, I made sure she was being looked after properly. In fact, throughout this period, it was never anyone else I was bringing harm to, only myself.

If ever I did go out, I'd convince myself I was going to have a good night, but I'd sabotage myself by doing stupid or reckless things, going places I shouldn't have, taking shit I shouldn't have been taking. Those nights, whenever they happened, were long. Endless hours in rooms surrounded by other people who were just as fucked up as me, all telling themselves this was a good time. It was like I was eighteen again. I was forever trying to chase and force that 'good time' feeling, but all I was doing was damaging myself. And yes, I wish I could have been the person to say, I don't need this drink, I don't need these drugs, I'm just going to enjoy the music. But when the people around me were all going one way, I found it hard to resist.

There were days when I felt suicidal, and there were a couple of occasions when things got too much and I tried to take my life. I'm not going into details on this; I have no wish to revisit that pain. Sometimes I look back and think, *Did I really do those things? Was I really there?* At the time, once my head told me there was a way out, it was all I could think about, and nothing could pull me out of it. That's the thing with me, if my mind sets me on a path, however bad that path might be, I have to keep following it. In the muddle of all these twisted thoughts, I'd ask myself how I got here and where my life was going, but I was in no fit state to answer either of those questions – they were just thoughts and sentences sent to torture me over and over again. Those questions always led me to another, darker question: *Why am I even here?* There were times when I wished the harm that I was inflicting on myself might take me away for good.

Now, I can safely say that that time and those thoughts feel like they were happening to a different person. It's yet another moment where I wish I could talk to my younger self, take her by the hand and tell her that however bad things seem now, it will all be OK. I feel blessed that I'm still here and still alive.

Back in those lowest moments, however, nothing felt OK. My mind was running riot in my head, and I was all over the place. Many people around me were telling me that I needed help, but in my mind they were trying to control me or make me behave myself. I resisted with everything I had. I didn't want to know. There were a few who thought I was attention-seeking, but that wasn't the case. The last thing I wanted was attention; I wanted to be behind closed doors, and on my own. To suffer in silence and solitude. That's the way I have always been. I can smile and laugh with you, then walk into a bathroom and cry my eyes out in private. But when I walk back out to face you again, you'd never know what had just happened.

For those reasons, I have always listened when someone tells me how depressed they are, or mentions harming themselves or suicide. You can never know how someone really feels, so labelling someone an attention-seeker is dismissive and dangerous. I'll always give these people the time of day.

Mostly, this period of my life is a bit of a blur now. A lot of dark, shapeless memories. There are things I look back on that send shivers through me. When I think, *God, did I do that? Is that how I was living my life?* I had such struggles, but I was always so terrible at accepting help.

The days I spent in bed not wanting to get up, shower or brush my hair or teeth now feel like unbelievable dreams. Those days when I only got up once it was dark to start the cycle of drinking and taking drugs all over again were all too real. I don't like the word 'regret' because I think we all go through things, and learning from them is much more valuable than regretting them. Still, there are many things I wish I'd done differently: time lying in bed with the curtains closed that I can never get back, times when I refused to sleep or eat properly, convincing myself I was enjoying myself when I was really just running on fumes.

I was so deep in depression I couldn't see a way forward. I cried about anything and everything. I hated myself and, therefore, believed that everyone else must hate me too. Was I screwing up the chance I had to be singing with the girls again? Were they going to abandon me? Everything was negative.

In the end, it came down to self-love, and I had none.

I do remember Keisha and Siobhan coming to my house, both looking like they thought someone was about to die. I realize now that someone was me. They told me that I needed to go somewhere to get help, and their voices joined the chorus of all the other voices of people close to me telling me the same thing. In the end, I knew they were right, so a joint decision was made.

The idea was that I would go to a hospital in London where I could get myself together again and dry out.

NINETEEN

I CRIED THE WHOLE WAY to the hospital. Saying I'd do it was one thing, but now it was real. Once again, the voice in my head was hard at work – *They're pressuring you, Mutya, you're being pressured into this. You're a grown woman, you should be at home.*

I walked into the place, pulling my suitcase behind me with my heart full of dread. I'd agreed to be there but, if I'm honest, I wasn't really doing it for me. In the end, I'd gone there for others. I'd gone along with the plan because if enough people were telling me I needed to be there, surely they must be right.

At the reception, I was greeted by people who looked like they'd been expecting me, which felt unsettling. There were a couple of big security guards standing in the reception too, and I thought, *There's no way I'm getting past those dudes.*

As I was shown to my room, I looked around me, thinking, *Where's the door that leads back to reception? Where's the exit?* It was like I was already pre-planning an escape route without having spent any time there.

This stay in hospital was to help me with a few things. Apart from trying to get on top of my depression, I had to withdraw from all the stuff I'd been putting into my body that was clearly taking its toll. This was a place where I was only allowed to see close family and a few friends, and even that was for a limited time only on certain days. For the most part I was on my own.

The mirrors were made of bendy reflective material that you couldn't break, and there was virtually no privacy. Someone was always checking on you and none of our doors closed and locked. The scariest thing about the place was how many kinds of fucked-up people were staying there, me included. Drug, sex and gambling addicts, among others, all in the one building. There was even a woman who was addicted to surgery. She had this immaculate-looking body, but the work she'd had on her face was very apparent: it had been cut and pulled until it was unrecognizable. You'd think I'd have had an affinity with her, having had some surgeries myself, but in some ways, I judged her. I looked at her and thought, *There's a lot going on there!* I wasn't there because of an addiction to surgery, so I didn't see myself as the same. I felt that I was different from all the other patients.

I know now that these unfortunate people were there for the same reason as me – to get well – but at the time it was hard for me to put that together in my head. As far as I was concerned, I was in a building full of crazy people. I wasn't like them. I couldn't be, right? I was given a handful of pills to take every night before going to bed. One of these was a sleeping tablet that would knock me out, and I always felt uneasy about the fact that my door had to remain slightly open and I would be unconscious, not knowing who might be coming in and out of my room.

There was a courtyard at the facility where you could smoke, which you had to get to by walking downstairs and through the basement. I did this often; it was my little bit of comfort and fresh air. When my friend Laura came to visit, she opened my

eyes to how vulnerable I was there. After smoking our cigarettes in among a colourful crowd of patients, we went back
upstairs to my room. When I looked at Laura, I noticed a look
of panic in her eyes.

'I don't want to go to that basement again,' she said. 'It's
fucking scary. I was looking at everyone, and they all look
fucking nuts.'

I thought about my being there, comparing myself to the
people we'd just seen. Surely, I wasn't the same as them? Laura
didn't seem to think so.

During our stay, there were all sorts of therapy groups and
classes available to us, but I wasn't interested. Although we were
all encouraged to take part, to sit down together and talk, nobody
was forced to do it, and I didn't want to. If I had to be there, I was
just going to do my time and get through it. I was going to do it
my way: alone. I stayed in my room as much as I could, avoiding
any group activities because I didn't want to be around all these
'crazies'. The only person I spoke to regularly was the Filipino
nurse who gave me my pills each night. I didn't even really know
what the tablets were for. Maybe I was told, but the information
didn't go in. As far as I was concerned, it was just more people
trying to control me.

When I heard there was an art class available, I wanted to
take part, but I didn't want to sit in a room with the other
patients. I asked if I could do the art in the privacy of my room
and the people at the facility agreed. At the time, it felt like the
best thing for me, but it was also an incredibly lonely existence.
I lived for the days Tahlia's dad would bring her up to visit
me, but even then I was always worried that being there might
be weird or scary for her.

The truth was, the other people in there were probably

looking at me like I was the crazy one. In the end, no one in that place was better than anyone else. We were all there for a reason. I just couldn't see that then, and spending any time with the other patients would mean having to face up to that fact. I still wasn't ready for that. I felt embarrassed, I was ashamed, and I was fighting the whole idea of being there.

One afternoon, I asked if I could go to the Tesco across the road from the facility to buy some snacks. I was told I could go but had to be accompanied by a nurse. I wasn't happy about it, but I was desperate to get out of the same four walls, so off we went. In Tesco, I walked around, grabbing a few bits and pieces while the nurse lingered behind me. When I got to the counter, the guy serving looked up with a smile.

'Oh wow, you're from the Sugababes, right?'

'I am, yeah,' I said, smiling back. 'How are you?'

I watched as his gaze fell on the nurse behind me, and the penny dropped.

'Ah, so you're there,' he said, gesturing towards the hospital.

It was clear he'd put two and two together. I was mortified. I wanted the ground to open up and swallow me whole. I left with my snacks and never went back, but over the next few days, I felt anxious. All it would take was this guy telling the press that he'd seen Mutya Buena accompanied by a mental health nurse and the news would be everywhere. *Look at her now, look at how far she's fallen . . .*

I could see it all in my mind's eye, and it made my stay there even more uncomfortable.

After the embarrassment of being recognized, my goal was to gain the trust of the staff. If I was going to stay inside the whole time, I needed things to feel a bit more relaxed. The security were on my arse the whole time and I wanted that to change. Some of the other patients had a bit more freedom, so why couldn't I?

One day, I asked if I could pop to the pie and mash shop to get some food, unaccompanied, and the nurse agreed. When that all went without incident, people started to trust me and I was gradually allowed off my leash a bit more.

On my twenty-seventh birthday, a few of my friends and family came with Tahlia, who was seven at the time. They brought a cake and we did our best to celebrate, but I just kept crying. I knew that soon they'd have to leave, and I wanted to leave with them. In the end, I had to stop my daughter from coming in because I was devastated every time she left and found it too upsetting.

A while after that family visit, I got even more depressed. I knew I needed to sort my life out and make changes, but I also knew I couldn't do it from there. I'd been there almost two months, but now I needed to get out. I was determined to.

After a few more weeks there, I was allowed to go outside the facility with Laura. By then, the staff trusted me, and they were more relaxed about me doing stuff without supervision. We ended up going to a bar, which, given I was meant to be sober, was not ideal. After a few drinks, I came to a big decision.

'I'm escaping,' I told Laura.

'What?'

'You heard me, I'm escaping. I'm getting out of that place.'

Somehow, I managed to get back to my room in good time that day, without anyone guessing what I'd been up to. I probably wouldn't have cared that much if I had been caught. I didn't want to be there anyway, so getting thrown out would have been a bonus. It didn't matter, though. I already had a plan in place.

I told Laura to come back for a visit as soon as she was next allowed, and I would be ready. She did just that, and again, I asked the staff if we could pop out for a while. Only this time, I wasn't coming back. I did a runner, with Laura as my getaway driver. It was so much of a dash that I had to abandon most of the possessions I'd gone in there with. As far as I know, they still have my suitcase at the hospital.

I was happy to be back home in Watford with my daughter, but there were a few raised eyebrows about my early departure from the facility. My family were upset that I'd given up and left. They knew I needed professional help, but now I'd removed myself from the care they thought I desperately needed, and they didn't know what to do next. That's one of the reasons I try never to feel sorry for myself. I had the support, it was right there for me to take, I just didn't accept it. Instead I chose to destroy myself, and I was doing a good job. Not long afterwards, I was drinking again and back to square one.

After going through all of it, I didn't really feel like my hospital stay had done me any good, but then again I'd never given it a chance. I would always encourage people to accept that kind of help or seek it out if they feel they need it. I'm not knocking it at all; I'm just saying it was probably a waste of time for me, because of where I was at that time in my life. You have to want to get better or it's not going to work. I just wasn't in that place yet. If nothing else, for me it was a clean moment, and it gave me a bit of time to reflect and gather my thoughts.

I'm thankful that, these days, issues around mental health are spoken about more freely and often. Things that were once shut away or swept under the carpet are taken seriously, and that can only be a good thing. In the past, I felt embarrassed about my depression and anxiety, which is part of the reason it was able to keep a grip on me for so long. Now, people feel more able to cry out loud, and to speak about what they're going through openly, even those in the public eye. That's another positive thing about social media. People who are going through a bad time have access to others who might be suffering in the same way. They can see themselves reflected back and know they're not alone.

Whenever I drive past that hospital now, it sends shivers through me. Every time I pass, I look up at the little window of the room I stayed in for all those weeks that barely opened, wondering who is there now and what they're going through. I almost have to pinch myself to accept that I was ever really there. How did I get so low? How could I have lost control like that?

In those moments, I make sure to mentally pat myself on the back and accept that I have been through so much and have come so far. It's easy to punish yourself for your past mistakes, but much harder to congratulate yourself for overcoming them.

TWENTY

I'D MISSED OUT ON SO much work while I was in the facility and even in the lead-up to being there. As far as I was concerned, the best thing for me was to get right back to it.

'Are you sure you should jump straight back into work, Mutya?'

That was the general feeling from everyone, but sometimes that's just what a person needs. It's definitely what I felt I needed. Though other aspects of my life were mentally draining me and pulling me backwards, Keisha and Siobhan were two girls I loved and trusted, trying to help pull me out of the shit time I was having. I knew that if this was going to work, I was going to have to kick myself up the arse and get it together. Being with the girls helped me a lot.

In May 2012, we were nominated for *Glamour* magazine's Band of the Year Award, along with Little Mix and Florence + The Machine, and at the end of the year we played *Ponystep Magazine*'s New Year's Eve party, performing 'Freak Like Me', 'New Year' and 'Overload'. It was the first time the three of us had performed together in a decade and quite the moment. It felt like things were moving and we were on a roll.

We'd already had a lot of material recorded by the time we signed to Polydor, having worked on tracks with Richard 'Biff' Stannard, Sia, Emili Sandé, MNEK, Shaznay Lewis and

Cameron McVey, who we used to work with in the old days. However, we all felt we still needed that killer first single, so we flew to New York to write alongside Dev Hynes, also known as Blood Orange and, before that, Lightspeed Champion. Dev had written and produced tracks with Britney Spears, Florence + The Machine, the Chemical Brothers, Kylie and even Mariah Carey – so he was a very cool person to write with.

The song that emerged from that session, 'Flatline', came together quite quickly on our first day in the studio. While Dev played around on the keyboard, we were vibing with ideas and melodies until we found things we all liked. Like most of the tracks on the album, we simply held our mics in the room and sang, passing the mic back and forth while the track played on a loop. None of the vocals were recorded traditionally in a booth. And there was none of that splitting us up and all recording different bits, like we did on some of our albums. No, this time it was similar to how we'd recorded *One Touch* all those years before. It felt simpler; purely about the music. As soon as the song started coming to life that day, we all knew it was special. By the end of the session, we had our first single.

For the video, we spent our own money and flew to LA. This turned out to be a great bonding time for us. We hung out, went to Universal Studios and just had fun together. We never really had the time to do that when we were on breakneck schedules as kids. The video, directed by fashion photographer KT Auleta, is a burst of sunshine. It starts with the three of us walking around Venice Beach among all that beautiful colour and personality and ends with us dancing in the desert as the sun sets over mountains. It felt like a nostalgic summer holi-day. On its release, despite rave reviews, 'Flatline' didn't make a mark the way I felt it should have. It reached number 14 in Ireland and 50 in the UK. It was disappointing, and I wondered if the fact that we were MKS and not Sugababes meant that people didn't recognize us. We were the same girls singing the same vocal harmonies, but it seemed the public weren't getting on board and taking us seriously.

Still, we carried on, with our first official headline gig at the Scala in August 2013, where we performed new songs and some of the classics. It felt wonderful to be performing with my girls again, but in some ways it was strange for me. I'd now been a solo performer for a long time; I'd forgotten what it was like to step out on stage flanked by two other women. Nevertheless, the fact that it was the two women I'd grown up and started my career with made it special. It felt important. It felt like a defining moment. And I wouldn't have it any other way.

In November of that year, we started the Sacred Three Tour, playing six dates across the UK. This felt very different to when we had gigged together as girls, certainly for me. I was more present, more in control. It was a vibe and we all caught it. The three of us all had the same goal: to make it work this time, and to enjoy it.

As a band, we were still raring to go, but because 'Flatline' had failed to hit the heights we'd all hoped for, Polydor didn't see our relationship moving forward, and to be honest, neither did we! At the time, they had a lot going on as a label. Girls Aloud were doing their massive comeback tour and releasing new music, and we wanted to be more of a priority than we were. We decided the best way forward was to take our songs back and move on. In the end, our relationship with Polydor was a fleeting one, over in the blink of an eye. The problem was, now we didn't feel like we had a platform from which to release our music. Although we continued gigging, the songs we'd worked so hard on would spend a long time in the wilderness.

Throughout this period, after my time in the hospital, I went from my terrible relationship with Pauly to another one which was even worse. One of my flaws is that I tend to jump quickly into relationships, even if I've only just come out of one. If I like someone, I give myself over, jumping in with both feet and, I suppose, hoping for the best. It's a bad trait, and things can get serious fast. It's not easy to write about because I don't want any of these people to take up space in my thoughts. Looking back, I feel like the mental health issues of these guys were as bad as, if not worse than, mine. I always seemed to attract men who liked to drink. Maybe that says something about me, but it was definitely the case. So, during the time when I should have been getting myself together and putting my energy into MKS, I was still drinking heavily. We're talking bottles at a time, and often it wasn't the good stuff.

My second relationship started very differently from the one with Pauly. Again, it's a fake name, but let's call him Alfie. When I think about these two men now, it feels like they were the same person in two different bodies. When I tried to step away from either of them, it was always cat and mouse, hide and seek. They'd come looking for me.

I met Alfie via Instagram; at first, he was a diamond, an absolute darling! He treated me like a princess, turning up with bags of designer clothes he'd randomly bought for me. Yes, Alfie had a bit of money and his own place, and I'd never had a guy go shopping and buy me nice things before. It was a bit of a shock at first, but after a couple of goes around, I started thinking, *Oh yes, I could get used to this!* Precisely what he did to get all this money was a mystery to me, and it's probably best left that way.

We dined out in nice places or he'd cook for me. We had fun together, and it felt like there was never a dull moment. After my horrible experience with Pauly, this felt comfortable and safe. It was all very hunky-dory . . . at least for a while. What I didn't realize at first was that Alfie was an alcoholic. And I don't mean just a party drinker: this dude could down an entire bottle of brandy and then move on to beer and a few bottles of prosecco. The seriousness of his drinking sort of crept up on me until one night he came back from the off-licence with twelve bottles of Stella and three bottles of prosecco. I asked him if I could have a bottle of Stella, and he looked at me angrily. 'I asked you if you wanted anything, and you said no. So no, you can't.' The thought of sparing one measly bottle of beer was too much for him. Until then, I just thought he liked a knees-up, but I realized then how bad it was. The thing is, I did nothing about it. If anything, I went along with it.

From early in our relationship, Alfie and I started drinking together. We'd drink at home and we'd also go out drinking in local pubs with friends. It would often start fine, with us having a good time, but the more alcohol he consumed, the more things would deteriorate. My thought was always, *Well, if you're going to get pissed and lairy, then I'm going to do it too.* I felt like if I was drunk, then his drunkenness wouldn't affect me. Of course, this was madness, but I wasn't in a good place, so this line of thought seemed perfectly logical to me at the time. *If he's going to be pissed, Mutya, you'd better be pissed too.* In so many ways, I was just adding to my troubles, but I wasn't in any fit state to see how my own behaviour was just making shit worse for the both of us.

The fights that happened in the fog of all this drinking were terrible. One night while we were out, Alfie shoved me into the road in front of oncoming cars, and I lay there in the road crying. I was lucky I wasn't injured or killed. On other occasions, he'd get angry and go for me, and I'd run away from him. For the next few hours, we'd play cat-and-mouse between cars and houses, with him trying to catch me. I'd run into a pub and hide, then sneak out when I thought he was gone. If he couldn't find me, he'd get in his car and drive around the streets while I crouched down, hiding behind cars, terrified. This happened several times during our relationship, but whenever things would get close to being too much, things would suddenly switch back, and we'd have fun together and everything felt fine again. On a good day, it would go back to the way it was at the beginning. He would shower me with gorgeous gifts and make a fuss of me. Those were some of the many times I pushed the bad shit to the back of my mind and pretended it would all be OK. I was always hopeful that things would get better. I needed them to. But they didn't.

Alfie was often violent while drinking, and once that started, it became a habit. He was a big guy, and his aggression was such that he once bit my hand so badly that it drew blood and I had to go to the hospital and have a tetanus shot. Even when he was staying at my mum's, we would fight and she would have to intervene.

'I'm not having it; this is not your house,' she would yell.

One night, he got angry and smashed a window outside her flat and I had to call the police to come and calm things down.

Even on holiday the madness continued. Alfie once visited the Philippines with my family and me. On that trip, we got into a fight where he tried to attack me on a fucking tricycle. (In the Philippines, motorized bikes with an attached passenger cab are a common form of transport.) It was only because my family were all military-based and were able to take control of the situation that he managed to avoid arrest. He was lucky. This wasn't the UK, and in the Philippines violence is not taken lightly, especially against women.

My dad was furious about it, and I was too. We'd travelled around the world to this beautiful country and brought our misery with us. Now even my safe haven wasn't safe any more. I think that was when I realized that he would never change, and I started to despise him.

I had a crazy cousin (no longer with us) who everyone was terrified of. He couldn't stand Alfie and had warned him not to hurt me. After that incident, I threatened to set my cousin on Alfie if he didn't stay in line while we were out there. He didn't care. The moment we were back in London, he went face-to-face with quite a few guys I knew and didn't seem to realize that he could end up getting hurt. His arrogance was so big that he thought he was invincible. He thought he was Superman.

Crazy shit, yes, but there was even crazier to come.

One terrible night, we went out separately in south London. I was in Streatham with one of my close friends while he was out drinking with his boys in another part of town. He planned to pick me up later, and we'd head back to north-west London together. However, when he arrived to collect me, he had a friend with him and they were both very drunk. Stupidly, I got into the car. I shouldn't have because I could see they were both fucking trashed, but I did. As soon as I slid on to the seat, his drunken friend started being rude to me, running off his mouth and insulting me like I was a piece of dirt. Alfie said nothing.

As we headed to an estate in Stockwell to drop off Alfie's

mouthy friend, he wouldn't shut up. As you can imagine, having had a few myself, I was giving as good as I got, but I probably should have kept quiet.

'Tell her to shut her mouth,' Alfie's mate said, but I was having none of it, and I was furious with Alfie for letting it happen.

After that, things escalated quickly. The friend started to get nasty and even threatened me with violence. Whether he would've actually gone through with it, I'll never know. By the time we reached the estate and pulled into the car park, I was screaming at him like crazy, but instead of helping me, Alfie started threatening me too. I couldn't believe it. It suddenly dawned on me how utterly out of it they both were – god only knows how much they'd had between them.

I tried to escape, but they wouldn't open the doors. By then, it was three a.m. and I was stuck in a car with these two nutters on a rough estate in Stockwell.

For what seemed like ages, they came at me, yelling and abusing me. I argued back, but I was scared. There was no one to turn to and nowhere to go. As feisty as I was, this was a step too far. I remember thinking, *This is the night. I'm going to die in this car.*

I was there for several hours. It was one of those situations where time became unreal because of the alcohol involved, and every thought and word was magnified. It must have been seven a.m. when things calmed down a bit, and they both got out of the car, leaving me shut inside. I sat there breathing hard and looking around me, not knowing what to do. My eyes went to the front of the car, and I realized the keys were in the ignition. Within seconds, I'd thrown myself into the driver's seat, sat down and turned the key. Suddenly, I was speeding away from them while they screamed at me to stop.

As I drove through the quiet streets, my phone rang constantly on the seat next to me. At one point, I answered, putting it on speaker, only to hear Alfie screaming like crazy.

'Bring back my fucking car now!'

I didn't know what would be scarier, going back and facing them or stealing his car and inciting even more of Alfie's rage later on. Something told me just to dump the car and run to the nearest cab office, but in the end, I decided to take the car back. Unbelievable, but that's how faulty my thinking was back then. I drove back into the dire situation I'd only just escaped from.

When I arrived back at Stockwell, there was more shouting and lecturing, but, in the end, Alfie and I got in the car and drove back to north-west London. Along the way, we passed a couple of police cars, and I wondered whether I should try to flag them down. But by then, I was so worn out and scared, I felt like I couldn't risk it. I just had to get home, and hope things would calm down. Eventually, we pulled up outside my mum's, where he dropped me off. It was over, at least for now.

Mum always knew what was happening, and I knew it upset her. She'd seen the occasional bruises, and she'd seen us fighting enough times. Everyone we knew had. I even had cause to call Tahlia's dad to help me out again one night, which was something I hadn't wanted to do the first time, let alone twice.

Despite all that, I stayed stuck in this terrible, destructive relationship. I was so down on myself at the time; I didn't think I deserved anything better. Yes, there were times when I sat there wracking my brain about how I could get out of it and escape him for good, but those thoughts never came to anything. It always felt too complicated and scary to contemplate. In my foggy mind, I thought he might come for me if I left him, beat me up or even kill me. So, I just stayed. It just went on and I put up with it. I was scared of how he might react, but I was also terrified of being alone.

It wasn't like I was helping myself either. I was still doing drugs sometimes and doing my work with MKS while trying to keep it all from the girls. I'd turn up to the studio, hurt and upset, but rather than levelling with them and telling them what I was going through, I made up stories to explain my moods or the way I looked. I can't tell you how many lies I made up to cover my shame, and the girls probably didn't believe most of them anyway.

It all changed one day when I went over to Alfie's house and found him in a strange mood. I couldn't put my finger on it, but I felt like something was going on with him. He was quiet and sheepish, which wasn't something I was used to, but I didn't dare question him in case we got into it.

I slept over at his place that night, and the following morning, as calm as anything, he said, 'Your Uber is on its way.'

'Oh, OK,' I said, surprised. 'So you're chucking me out?'

He shrugged, but I didn't ask any further questions. Instead of arguing about it, I went with it. I simply got ready, waited for the Uber to turn up and got in it. As the car pulled away, I wondered what the hell was going on with him. Had he got another woman going over? Had he finally realized what a shit show of a relationship this was? I assumed the first, but I didn't care. I went home that day and never heard from him again.

After that, my friends didn't hold back in telling me what they thought. They couldn't believe I hadn't seen what they saw; they said that I only saw what I wanted to see. They were right. I'd never had a guy treat me like he had when we first got together, and for a long time, I was blinded by that.

I never want to be in a relationship like that again, and I won't let it happen. I have too much self-respect now. And my head is clear!

Unfortunately, though, the ghost of that relationship hung over me. I didn't rush into another one, but when one eventually came along, it suffered because of what I'd been through.

Here and now, I have to give myself credit for coming through all that. Ultimately, I had to remember who I was and set my boundaries. I look back on that period as a nightmare that I've put behind me. I am not in contact with those men, and I make sure they don't even pop up on my social media feed. These days, I'm much more aware and careful about who I lie down with. Intimacy with the devil is not an option any more.

TWENTY-ONE

UNFORTUNATELY, I TURNED TO SELF-HARM again during that dark period. Wrongly, I felt like I didn't have people to turn to, so that became my go-to, and it got worse as time went on. At times of stress, I would take a knife or simply break something and cut myself.

After it happened, I'd always have to deal with the harsh reality of what I'd done. While other women were walking around in summer with their arms out looking pretty, I had to cover up. Hide my shame. I couldn't stop because, like alcohol and drugs, it had become my way to blot out reality.

I was watching a piece about it on TV once, where someone asked a woman who self-harmed why she did it.

'Because I feel like I can breathe,' she said.

I remember thinking, *Oh my god, that's me!* That's exactly how I felt about harming; that it let me breathe. It gave me relief.

But with that breath came pain and even secret hospital visits to have my arm stitched up.

A few months ago, I saw a young girl whose body was a roadmap of cuts and wounds – like tiger stripes all over her body. What fascinated me about this young woman was that she didn't try to hide any of it; she seemed proud of her scars, which maybe told a thousand stories. Looking at her, I wanted to hug her. The idea that she would feel such aggression towards herself was both heartbreaking and shocking. People who do that to themselves don't usually want to die; they're not trying to kill themselves: they're doing it because it seems like the only option, the only way to find relief. And yes, that sounds crazy to other people, but often it feels like the only solution to whatever they're going through.

Stress and anxiety can be a killer, but while some people go for a run, listen to music, smoke a cigarette or maybe grab a coffee, people like me and this young girl often take a different road. In those days, when so much anger and pain came from within me, I'd have loved to have woken up and thought, *Fuck this, I'm going for a fucking long walk*, but that wasn't how my psyche worked. Thankfully, I have much healthier ways of dealing with those emotions now.

Looking at this battle-scarred young woman, I could only hope that whatever she'd been going through, it was all behind her. I hoped she was in a better place now, although I couldn't possibly know.

I had another shock in store in 2014, and this time it wasn't something I brought about myself. When you're self-employed and in the entertainment industry, there is a lot of official and legal stuff to juggle. You have to put your faith in managers, lawyers and accountants, and trust that they will do the best job and work in your best interests. I was paying the people who worked for me good money to do just that, but I was badly let down.

I was at home one evening when there was a knock on the door. When I opened it, I was confronted by a woman holding a folder, flanked by two burly guys who looked like security men.

'We're here on behalf of Her Majesty's Customs and Excise,'

she said. 'Are you aware that you owe one hundred thousand pounds in unpaid tax?'

To say I was stunned was an understatement. I opened my mouth, wondering what this woman expected me to do. Did she think I was going to pull a hundred grand out of my arse or pop upstairs and fetch it from my knicker drawer?

'What do you mean, one hundred thousand pounds? How is that even possible?'

The rest of the conversation was a blur, but it involved the woman telling me how long I had to settle this bill before all sorts of bad shit fell into my lap.

When I spoke to someone at the tax office the following day, I told them I was confused.

'I pay accountants to do my tax returns and handle my tax bills, so how is it possible I owe all this money? I haven't had a single letter sent to my house about this. How is that possible?'

Of course, there had been letters. Lots of letters. But they'd all gone to my accountants' office and I hadn't been told about a single one of them.

It got worse. Not only had my taxes not been handled correctly, but my accountants had made financial agreements I knew nothing about.

'There's an agreement to pay this debt – fourteen thousand pounds a month,' the man on the phone told me.

'What? Hold tight! There's no way I can afford that at the moment. Who agreed to that, and how did I know nothing about any of this?'

'Well, that's what's been agreed by your accountants, and that's what's expected,' he said. 'Perhaps you shouldn't have left this all in your accountants' hands. In future, you need to be more on top of it yourself.'

'I didn't even see the letters,' I argued, but there was no point.

Everything I said went unheard. It even reached the point where he checked the address of where the letters had gone, confirming that none had come to me personally. Still, this was a done deal. There was nothing I could do, and a bankruptcy case was looming.

Thankfully, I owned a couple of properties at the time, the one I lived in and another I rented out. The last thing I wanted to do was sell off my assets, but this was a huge amount of money, and it was the only way I could pay it off.

Because the situation was so complex and had been going on for so long without my knowledge, time ran out and the courts declared me bankrupt. Anyone who has gone through bankruptcy will know that your hands are tied once it happens. You can't do anything because you have no credit rating or financial freedom. I had to go through all these doors and sit through meeting after meeting about my situation, feeling like shit. My company was liquidated and my properties were sold. Meanwhile, I felt like everyone was looking down at me the whole time. I couldn't cope. If I'd been depressed before, this situation plunged me even deeper than I'd ever known.

Before I knew it, the story was all over the papers – the press had a field day! 'Former Sugababes Mutya Buena is declared bankrupt!' 'Mutya bankrupt after being chased for unpaid tax.' 'Former Sugababe Goes Bust!' The articles added my name to a list of other nineties and noughties celebs who'd suffered the same fate. The pain lasted well beyond my own moment. In every subsequent article about any other celebrity's financial troubles, my name was repeatedly dragged up again. I had to relive this over and over. It didn't matter that I'd paid the bill as soon as possible or that it wasn't my fault it had happened in the first place. No one seemed interested in that part of the story, and those who did mention it used phrases such as '*Buena claims it was an administrative error*,' – like I was simply making excuses. Everyone was quick to announce my bankruptcy, but no one reported when I'd paid the debt. It was frustrating and humiliating, and I had no control over any of it. That was the worst part about it. Not the debt or the bankruptcy hearing, or even the shock of finding out that my accountants had fucked up so badly without me knowing. It was also the shame, the fact that I was seen as this washed-up, broke former pop star. All my business was out there for the UK – for the world – to see. It was so embarrassing, I didn't even want to leave the house. In fact, at one point, I didn't leave the house for about three weeks because I thought everyone I walked past was looking at me, thinking the same thing.

I was angry too. Angry that someone I had entrusted to manage my finances had let me down. Angry that no one wanted to hear the truth. I wanted them to publish the full story, to apologize and say they'd got it wrong. Of course, that was never going to happen. They weren't interested in facts. I was just going to have to live with it, and when you're a proud person, as I am, that's fucking hard to swallow. I worried about my family too. I imagined my daughter being teased at school because of her mother's public failure; my parents still having to support me at the age of almost thirty.

To add the cherry on the cake, there was no accountability for the people who'd screwed up my finances in the first place. They just walked away, leaving me to mop up the mess. Looking back, I wish I'd had it in me to fight more, but I didn't. I was so embarrassed by it all that I couldn't even bring myself to try to pursue justice. I just wanted it all to be over.

After I was declared bankrupt, I moved back in with Mum and Dad. I had to because my credit rating was so completely fucked that I couldn't even rent a place. When I finally was able to rent somewhere, it wasn't ideal. Although it was in north-west London and close to Tahlia's school, it was on a main road, so every time I stepped out of my front door, I was in the thick of lots of noise and commotion. At that point, I was still carrying a lot of baggage and embarrassment about what had happened to me, so I found being out in public quite difficult. I struggled with crowds, feeling like everyone was staring at me or talking about me. I knew a lot of people in the area, which didn't help with the feeling that I was constantly being judged. I just wanted to be anonymous. I'd been a successful recording artist with number-one records to my name, and here I was starting from scratch, having fallen on my arse. As far as I was concerned, that's all people saw when they looked at me, and all they said when they spoke about me.

I noticed some people I'd once called friends distancing themselves from me. It even got back to me that certain people said that I wasn't doing anything with my life and they didn't want to associate with that.

God, that period was so full of ups and downs – mostly downs – trying to make myself better and then feeling good about something for a hot second before the next thing knocked me flat again. Each time I went down, it felt further than before and harder to climb back up again. It was as if I was being dragged around from place to place, doing the day-to-day things I needed to without any command over my body or mind.

I didn't want to die, but some days I also couldn't face living. I admit I did have suicidal thoughts again, but the thought of leaving my family and not seeing my daughter grow up were the things that always pulled me back.

Over the years, I've heard many people say that people who take their own lives are selfish, but if a person can no longer live in their own skin or things feel so bad that they can't see a way out, it might seem like their only way of achieving peace or shutting down the noise. There is always a better way – choosing to live is better – but when someone feels they have nowhere left to turn, they're not being selfish. They are in despair.

It's only recently, ten years on, that things have started to return to normal with my finances. My credit rating has been restored, and I've been able to think about buying a new house. As far as paying my taxes is concerned, I'm on it like Sonic. I don't even want to be a day late with those payments. I had to learn the hard way, but I have indeed learned from it.

TWENTY-TWO

EVENTUALLY, I WAS ABLE TO rent somewhere a lot quieter and I started feeling better. This was a place where there was community and I had lovely neighbours, a place where I could hopefully get back on my feet. I was starting again, but this time things were going to be very different. They had to be.

I believe the biggest thing that helped me out of that dark time was focusing on myself and throwing myself into work with the girls. It had helped get me out of funks before and this was no different. I hated letting people down, and deep down I knew that if things continued the way they were, it would be a disaster for all concerned.

Going through bankruptcy meant I had to start over from scratch, so I applied that to every aspect of my life. I calmed down with the drinking and stepped away from the toxic relationships I'd been in, and I was able to show up for the girls and do the work I needed to do. Part of that meant reclaiming our name: Sugababes.

I'm not going to go into the legalities of getting our name back; suffice to say that there was a lot of back-and-forth with previous management, and it took a while and a lot of paperwork. As far as I was concerned, the three of us had started that brand and worked our arses off to help make it what it was. Yes, there had been various line-ups, but after the final original member had left and no one was using it, why shouldn't the original members take it on? We deserved it, surely.

Still, the process was a struggle and took a long while. It wasn't fun. Eventually, though, an agreement was reached, and we did it. Finally, we were allowed to work under our original name, and it made us all very happy. This would change everything. We were Sugababes again.

By then, we'd been back together for about eight years, and it had been quite a journey. After all the initial excitement of our reunion, a record deal that came and went, a tour and an unreleased album, time had marched on. Despite gigging as MKS, we hadn't released any new material besides 'Flatline'. Some of the other tracks we had recorded were leaked online, which didn't help, and we had spent time in the studio recording more, but it all took time. So, when DJ Spoony asked us to feature on his cover version of Sweet Female Attitude's 'Flowers' at the end of summer 2019, we jumped at it.

This would be the first time we would release something under the newly reclaimed Sugababes name. Spoony's was a beautiful version of the classic song, with lovely string orchestrations, sprinkled with our distinct three-part harmonies. It was a great match, and when we performed it live on *The Graham Norton Show,* the penny finally seemed to drop with the public. People saw us together, under the name Sugababes, and it was, *Fuck, the girls really are back together!* Suddenly, people were into it and jumping on the hype. It was funny because we'd been back for a few years by then, but having the name everyone recognized was what sealed the deal.

Finally, on 24 December 2022, we released the album we'd recorded almost nine years before – *The Lost Tapes*. It was an independent release, but we were over the moon to finally get it out there. It felt like a long time coming and we were so proud of ourselves.

In many ways, it was as if we were starting all over again, building up our fanbase and asking them to have faith and believe in us. One thing we didn't want was just to be seen as a reunion band, just playing an endless round of greatest hits shows and nostalgia festivals. I'm not putting those shows and bands down, far from it, but we didn't feel like we were there just yet. We still had something new to offer and wanted to keep moving forward. There was still a distance to go. Sometimes, I'd see shows with great line-ups and think maybe we should have been doing them, but at the same time, I was very happy and grateful for the gigs we were playing.

Playing at Glastonbury would probably be one of the highlights of any music artist's career, and I have been lucky enough to do it three times with Sugababes. The first time was with Keisha and Heidi during the group's second line-up. On that occasion, we played the Pyramid Stage – one of the first all-girl bands to do it!

But since getting the original band back together, we've played the festival twice more – once in 2022 and, more recently, in 2024. The funny thing about Glastonbury is I was always worried that nobody would turn up – yes, even now! I get the worst stage fright and nerves before doing a show like that. You'd think I'd be used to it, but sometimes I'm a nervous wreck before we go on. Clearly, I was way off!

In 2022, we played on the Avalon Stage, the area of which was supposed to accommodate up to 3,000, but eventually, the police had to restrict entry because of safety concerns. There were just too many people who wanted to see us, trying to scramble over gates and squeeze into the space. Last year, we were upgraded to the much larger West Holts Stage, but the area still became overwhelmed by the size of the crowd trying to see us. Ultimately, once again the organizers had to close the area, to prevent any more people from getting in. According to the Glastonbury app, 90,000 people wanted to see us, but the West Holts Stage could only accommodate up to 35,000. It was absolute mayhem!

As for that 2024 performance, we were in and out so fast it made our heads spin. We had to be done in just over an hour because we had a private gig in Morocco the following day and needed to be on a six a.m. flight. Still, walking out on that stage in front of all those people was incredible. There were heads and bodies as far as the eye could see. As hard as I tried, I couldn't quite figure out where the crowd ended; it just went on for ever. It was beautiful, especially singing songs that are so well known and have been around for so long. 'Overload' is turning twenty-five years old this year!

Regarding what songs we perform, we do Sugababes songs up to when Keisha left, which is all of the big ones, including the six number ones. The great thing about the Sugababes' legacy of music is that we get to enjoy it all because, at one time or another, together or separately, we were a part of it. Having left after the band's first album, Siobhan had the most material to learn, but she has put her distinctive mark on those songs and embraces them as her own. We've all had our individual journeys, so we celebrate them all.

We also love performing songs from *The Lost Tapes* album,

and at Glastonbury we did our most recent single, 'When The Rain Comes', and the crowd loved it. When it comes to festivals, I always feel that the audience want to hear classic hits – that's what they come for! So it was extra special to see such a strong reaction to our new music. I see many comments online about us changing things up and wanting to see us doing something fresh.

'Love the sets, love what you do, but you need to bring some new music out.'

We all agree, and it's something we're working on. There are definitely new things to come, so watch this space!

It still amazes me that people want to turn up and see us after all this time, and playing Glastonbury, particularly coming from the background and area we all do, is such a blessing. We'd fought for so long to get our name back and be recognized as the Babes once again, so it felt surreal that the crowds were there waiting for us. There are so many other bands from the era when we started who've fallen by the wayside, but somehow we've come through and still get to shine. And as Keisha loves to say, 'We're not old – we're just below Beyoncé and slightly above Rihanna!'

And she's right – there's still so much time and more for us to do. We want to work more in the States and go to Asia. We have followings in so many countries, and we want to reach all of them. It feels so good to be dreaming big again!

These days when we're on the road, we might be on a bus for hours. It's always a very relaxed vibe now, lots of talking and laughing, watching films or playing games together – and there's usually a bottle open! Sometimes I look around and just marvel at how far we've come.

The fact that we still get to do shows like Glasto, the Mobos and the Brits after all these years and after everything we've been through as a group, and individually, is something I will never take for granted. I let so much pass me by when I was young and first experiencing everything, but not now. Now, I appreciate every second of everything we do.

TWENTY-THREE

EVER SINCE MY FIRST EXPERIENCE with plastic surgery, I was always keen to make more 'improvements'. After my successful first breast surgery, I decided I might try something else, so I got my butt done – the full Kim Kardashian! This was my first trip to a clinic in Turkey, but it was just the first of many. I didn't even do a huge amount of research when I was looking for a Turkish clinic: I simply googled and then went with the one who got back to me, sounded friendly and seemed like they knew what they were talking about.

What's that expression? 'You're not ugly; you're just poor.' Well, I guess I subscribed to that. If I had the money to fix something and improve myself, I would do it!

At first, I told myself I was just doing it to make myself feel better – and that's what I truly believed – but looking back, there was an element of ego involved. I was trying to impress people, which is never the best reason to do anything.

The thing about surgery is that it can be addictive. For me, it became habitual, that constant quest to improve myself. When you have the double whammy of an addictive personality and not always liking yourself or not being kind to yourself, it can get out of control. That's what happened to me. I've spent many years finding faults in my body and trying to correct those perceived faults and imperfections.

It was a case of one thing leading to another, and I would spend hours on the net looking at what was possible. I'd see something and think, *Yeah, I could do with that. That would make me feel better about myself.* And it did, for a while.

When I first had liposuction, for instance, I thought, *Ooh, everything looks really smooth.* Then a few months later, that happiness would wear off and I'd zone in on something else I wanted to change, and the cycle would start all over again.

There was always another procedure, something more to fix. The trouble is, when you're in that mindset the whole time, you're constantly chasing something that's ultimately unobtainable – perfection.

There was one particular clinic that became a place where I felt safe. I felt the people there would make me look and feel better. It was four big houses joined together, and people from all over the world travel there for their facelifts, hair transplants, breast enlargements and everything else you can think of. I was so comfortable with the clinic that I could simply WhatsApp them and ask when they could fit me in, which was much too easy for someone like me. By then, the fear I'd had with my first procedure was long gone. I even started to enjoy the process of having anaesthetic and drifting off to sleep. I'd fly in on a Monday morning and be in surgery on Tuesday. I'm a person who doesn't like to wait, so that suited me fine. I was lucky finding that facility, because from what we all now know, they're not all as professional and careful as the one I chose. Cosmetic surgery of any kind is not something you should undertake without a lot of research.

There have also been times when I've been booked to have a procedure but then haven't got on the plane because someone close to me warned me, 'Don't do it!' I think some of my friends thought I didn't need surgery, and perhaps had never done anything like that themselves. The trouble was, they couldn't see what I was seeing. They weren't feeling what I felt. Sometimes, they were probably right. I didn't fucking need it; if I really wanted it, I did it anyway. Yes, there might be a few I wish I hadn't gone through with, but I will have to live with them. It's not for everyone.

As you can imagine, it's not a cheap obsession either! But when I've been lucky enough to have the money, surgery often seemed like a reasonable thing to spend it on. There was always some kind of 'special offer' on the go with the Turkish clinics, which was a good way to justify to myself what I was doing. There were even payment plans for those who didn't have as much money.

From my breasts downwards, there's not much of me that's gone untouched – back, thighs, stomach. Aside from a bit of Botox and lip filler, the one thing I never had surgery on was my face, but it's certainly crossed my mind. For a while, I considered having a 'fox eye', where the outer corner of the eye is lifted to a slight angle, creating an arch. It's a bit of a mini lift. When I mentioned this to my mum, she pointed out that, being of Asian descent, I already had beautifully shaped eyes. Good old mums. They'll always think you look beautiful, no matter what.

Things have changed now, but I won't pretend that I have vanquished the perfection dragon and left my pursuit behind. Sometimes, I scroll my social feed to find mean or critical comments about the way I look. I might have ninety-nine positive comments, but if there's one negative one, I will often fixate on that. Initially, I'll think, *You cheeky bastard, who are you to comment on the way I look?* But in the back of my mind, that thought will stay with me for the whole day and get me down. Even on days when I'm busy and feeling good, the comment will go round and round in my head, and I'll find myself cringing and stressing over it. I'll end up going back to a post repeatedly to make sure there are no more negative comments, deleting any little thing I don't like, feeling embarrassed and ashamed.

I'm sure if I was advising somebody else, I would tell them, 'Just ignore the fuckers!' I wish it were that easy for me. My overactive brain can remember every mean comment that's been written about me. It's all been saved, like some mental scrapbook of negativity.

Most of the online hate I suffer comes from men. I'm used to seeing comments from women and girls telling me how amazing I look, but some guys can't seem to keep their negative thoughts to themselves.

It makes me start looking at myself and wondering what I could get done to fix the problem. Yes, even now it still happens, although I'm nowhere near as obsessive about that stuff as I was. It hasn't gone away, though. I'm still quietly looking at ways to improve my body. The problem is, I've not quite healed from within, and until that happens I will always feel like I should be perfecting what's on the outside. And as weird as it sounds, there's still a part of me that likes the idea of being gently sent to sleep, and then waking up a new person.

One of the things that's slowed me down is that as I've got older, surgery has become a lot scarier. The last procedure I had, in May 2023, brought complications. I started having panic attacks as I came round from the anaesthetic, and my blood pressure went sky high. I noticed during my recovery that the nurses were being extra vigilant, checking up on me much more than usual.

It put me off to a degree, but not completely. The fear of what might happen hasn't quite been enough to deter my need to constantly upgrade my looks, although it's calmed it down considerably. It's hard to ignore some of the horror stories you hear about things going wrong.

There's a lot to consider before going under the knife – the cost, the time it takes and most importantly your safety. You have to research, listen to recommendations and know exactly what the procedure entails and who is doing it. I would also remind anyone who's thinking about surgery that it's not a miracle cure, especially as you get older. If you have something snipped, tweaked or changed, you have to maintain it. There's no point in having fat removed and then thinking you can eat whatever you want and stay the same.

That's one of the reasons I have made other, more natural, manageable changes, which have made a huge difference. I don't drink alcohol like I used to. My drinking is saved for special occasions, restaurants and girls' nights out. I've also changed my diet. Gone are the days when I'd snack on KFC and all the unhealthy stuff. I've cut down on rice too – I was brought up eating loads of it, which was often a factor in my gaining weight. These days, I'm a lot more mindful about how I treat my body. I try to treat myself with respect. As much as I still sometimes feel the urge to improve my body, I know that the safest way to look and feel good is to do it naturally.

TWENTY-FOUR

WRITING THIS BOOK WAS NEVER about a big, explosive exposé or me feeling sorry for myself. For me, it was about being real with myself, celebrating the good things and people in my life, and accepting and being honest about the bad. Every day now, I try to be positive. Yes, there are still people and situations out there that aren't good for me, but I'm not so young and naive any more that I let those people and situations get close.

Recently, I've realized how important it is to surround myself with my own good energy. What I don't need is people around me who might threaten that. I have always fed off the energy of others, so if someone is having issues that might intrude on my thoughts and feelings, I try to stay away from them as much as possible. By the same token, I stay away from anyone who wants to party like I used to, or who tries to push their drama my way.

Because of this, I have had to let go of quite a few people I might once have called friends, and the result is that I feel so much better these days. I don't hear people talking about others badly, and I don't hear gossip or negativity. It's never a good thing anyway because if a person is talking shit to you about someone, you can be sure they're talking shit about you to someone else!

Not everyone I let go was a bad person, far from it; they just weren't the right people to have in my life. Moving on from them was one of the most significant steps in my recovery and my becoming the person I am now.

These days, I'd rather see the faces of my family members than I would anyone else's.

In the past, I often went out of my way to keep other people happy; it was just myself I didn't care about. Now, I've learned that I need to make myself happy, first and foremost. It's not selfish; it's necessary. The people I love could never be happy while I was the way I was. In the end, it had to start with me.

For all the people I had to leave behind, though, there are some friends that have come from the most unexpected places who have stayed with me through thick and thin. Funnily enough, some of the closest female friends I have now are people I met at various raves over the years. It may have been on the dancefloor of a club, through mutual friends, or even in the toilets. Any girl will know, the loos were always a great place to have a chinwag and talk shit to complete strangers. We'd all be as high as a kite, telling one another, 'Oh, I love your shoes' or 'Your hair looks amazing, who did it?' or the classic 'You should dump him!' There's no ego boost like the one you get from those random girls.

There was one girl I used to see very regularly, Melissa. We'd had a dozen casual chats in various loos across town; I always seemed to bump into her while I was out. There was one night out, at a club in Ealing where great DJs played the best house music, where she invited to me to join her at a new spot.

Before I knew it, I was hurtling across town in a car, with no idea where I was going. Was I being kidnapped here? As

Melissa chatted away to me, I was thinking, *I don't really know you. You could be abducting me.*

We ended up having the most fantastic time together, and never stopped talking after that. Over time we became great friends. She's a good and kind-hearted person, and stood by me when my life was in pieces. Some of my other friends at the time, the same ones who abandoned me when things got rough, treated her badly. They even stole from her at one point. But even through all of that, her friendship never wavered. At a time when I was being taken advantage of, she taught me what true friendship meant.

We only got closer as we entered adulthood. We both had young daughters, and I'd often take them with me to various premieres and events I got invited to. From the age of three, our daughters have grown up together, and they are also great friends. Even now, they fall asleep on FaceTime together some nights. It makes me smile to see it. All this from getting into a car with a random girl and going to Brixton, all those years ago.

The women I'm friends with now are happy for me and supportive of my choices. They're not looking to take from others because they're all big thinkers and go-getters themselves and they have their own stuff going on. Melissa has her own business, working with the NHS in mental health. Another friend, Natania, has her own catering company. Zara has her own beauty business, and then there's Krystal, who's one of the biggest go-getters I know! She's another person I met randomly, through a guy that neither of us speaks to any more. The guy might be history, but Krystal and I really are like sisters, and I have such admiration for her. Not long after we first met, she called me up one day and asked, 'What are you doing?'

'Nothing much,' I said. 'Why? What's happening?'

'Why don't you come over? I'll cook some food and we'll have some drinks and chill?'

That's very grown up, I thought, *but why not?* Once again, on my way there in the car I had this weird feeling that this might be some kind of set-up, or that I was being used. I was so used to being led on and let down by people that these kinds of thoughts always came into my mind. Here was someone who was making an effort with me, and I couldn't help but be suspicious. I just wasn't used to friends offering me anything without expectations.

We ended up having the time of our lives together. Krystal made fried chicken and we sipped champagne. It was a lovely evening where the drinks flowed and the two of us got to know one another. Krystal was someone who didn't have a lot of other female friends, but she seemed to like and trust me, and our friendship grew from that. From that evening onwards, we were almost inseparable.

Krystal ended up moving away to work in Dubai for the next three years and really made a success of it. I was sad that my friend had gone of course, but more than anything, I was so proud of her. This is what I love about women like her and why I call her my sister. She's so determined and motivated, always going after what she wants. She made her dreams happen.

Another friend, who is also like a sister, is Anupa. We've been through a lot together over the years, experiencing ups and downs at the same time, sitting at opposite ends of the sofa playing games on our phones. During COVID, we were often in a bubble together.

Recently, she came over with her new baby, and I felt so happy for her. We talked about our many wild nights and how things have changed for both of us.

'Doesn't it feel good to wake up in the morning, knowing you've got a whole day ahead of you, rather than the days when we woke up and couldn't even face daylight?' I said to her.

'And how good is it not feeling rubbish all the time?' Anupa added.

She was right. She always was. It was Anupa who would be there for my low points and, no matter what, would always show up at my front door when I needed help. She always understood what I was going through.

And I can't not mention Nicky, my bestie who has been there for me for many years. We've travelled all over the world together, from Barbados to Amsterdam, Vegas to New York. We've seen it all and I just love her to bits.

This strong group of women are now all friends with one another, so we can all go out and celebrate our successes together. And there's never a time when someone doesn't want to contribute. We all pay our way or treat one another in turn, and in the clubs, we're not sitting at a man's table waiting for him to buy us drinks – we have our own table, and we buy the drinks!

I've surrounded myself with this group of beautiful women who empower one another, who love and respect one another and who lift each other up. We send each other positive messages: 'Have a blessed morning!' 'Enjoy your day, queen!' 'Have a fabulous week!' Where there used to be gossip and drama, there's now vibrancy, love and positivity. That's all I've ever wanted from my friends. It's changed my life, and it's how it should be.

There are other areas of my life where I have better people around me too. I've finally found managers who are looking out for my interests before anything else. For the last few

years, I've been working with JAW Management, which is run
by two strong, amazing women, Nicole and Nicky. They're not
the same team that manages the Babes, but a small bespoke
agency that acts as personal management for everything I do
outside the band.

Nicole and Nicky came to me when everything had gone
very quiet in my career. I was lost and didn't really know what
I was going to do next. As far as they were concerned, I had a
lot of untapped potential and they were going to make things
happen. They believed in me at a time when I wasn't even sure
if I believed in myself any more, and out of our partnership,
so much has come. Back then, the team at JAW were great at
keeping me 'current' and out there, getting me all sorts of TV
work to keep me busy.

They're now also helping me work on ventures outside of
music. I'm developing a line of wigs and hairpieces with their
help. They got me my book deal, and we're constantly working
on thoughts and ideas for the future. I trust them, and I'm very
grateful to them because they didn't just swoop down during
the peak of my success when things would have been easier.
They showed up when I needed them and they did the hard
work. Under their guidance, I started to get back out there and
earn a living! They've been such a big part of the last five years,
and it feels good to have people around me that genuinely
want the best for me.

Letting myself be happy was a big part of my healing process.
The other thing that got me through was never feeling sorry
for myself. However bad I thought things were, I knew that
a lot of it was self-inflicted, and I also knew that some people
had it worse than me. Much worse. Many wouldn't have had
the support system I was lucky enough to have, the voices of

loved ones telling me, 'We're here for you, we love you.' With their help I kept some of my darkest moments out of the press, which I'm so grateful for.

It was a bittersweet situation sometimes. I had this amazing network of people around me, but I was still intent on ruining it all. That was on me. That was my fault. I didn't need any outside influences destroying my life; I was doing a great job of it all on my own.

Right now, I'm happier than I've ever been, but just a few years ago I'd never have believed it was possible. The struggle to get where I am started when I was a teenager and has lasted for the majority of my life. Time and time again, I tried to make myself better and pull myself out of the cycle I was trapped in. I've managed it now, but boy did it take for ever.

The biggest battle I've had in my life has been with my own mind. Over the years, I've often wondered how I'm still here with this troubled soul I'm carrying around. My demons have tried to defeat me so many times, especially during those days of despair and sadness. Those days of not waking up till the evening, not eating properly (or sometimes not even remembering whether I'd eaten or not). That life feels a million miles from where I am now, waking up every day at 4 a.m. and patting myself on the back to remind myself how well I'm doing and have done. Now, I've found peace, and I've learned to love myself. I feel I've been truly blessed.

It took a lot of soul-searching to turn things around. For one, it took me picking up my Bible, feeling like I needed God in my life to help me through. Before I did anything each morning, I asked God and the universe to please make my day a bit better than the one before.

I'm not big into meditation, but I have always believed in the universe holding possibility. I'm a person who sees 11:11 and thanks the universe. For me, words were the key to tapping into that; speaking my wants and desires out loud and manifesting good things became so important to me.

There was also a practical side to all this. I had promised myself that at a certain age, I would stop using and doing things that were harming my body – and I did. I limited my drinking and cut out all the other stuff. I could have been swayed a few years ago if someone pushed me, but that's no longer the case. The voices in my head telling me to get wasted or to cut myself have quietened. I pat myself on the back for that. I'm proud because the idea of hurting myself never enters my head now. And for anyone who has been through something similar and come out the other side, you should applaud yourself too and remember how strong you are. Don't look back and think about how you used to be; celebrate who you are now and look forward. That's what I do every day because I want to be proud of my body. I want to be on a beach showing it off. I want to get my arms out. Sure, I still want my skin to be clear, my legs to look silky and my boobs to be perky. To want all that and feel comfortable about going after it, I've had to work through a lot, and that's an ongoing process.

Sometime in the future, I'd like to talk to kids in schools about some of the issues I've dealt with in my life, particularly around self-harm. I think my experiences could help others because I come from a non-judgemental place of knowing and understanding. I could listen to and understand someone's reasons for doing what they do, but also offer alternative coping methods. I think that would be a beautiful thing to do, and I would love to make it happen.

There are so many kids out there who think they're alone,

but the truth is, they just don't know where or who to turn to. They might be stuck in a situation or a household where no one gives a shit, but there are other people and places out there that can help. They just need the information and a non-judgemental ear.

I feel lucky that I'm still here singing, as I have been from such a young age, and that I've managed to come from losing everything to where I am now, where life finally feels comfortable. I'm not rich in money, but I am in heart, and I have many people to thank for that, including the two amazing women I share a stage with, Siobhan and Keisha.

These days, my working life feels like it's come full circle. I'm back with my original Sugababes, who I love to bits, and I get everything I need from the work we do together. I no longer need the extra buzz of a crazy social life on top. Now when I go out, I usually want to come home after an hour because I get bored. These days, I am very good at saying no. If something sounds like it's not up my street, then I'll politely decline. I don't feel I'm missing out if I'm not there. I come out of my house for the right reasons, and if I do go out, I know when to leave and come home.

It's funny, but I have so many bottles of wine and champagne in my kitchen right now that have been sitting there for ages because I simply don't drink at home any more. The idea of sitting down in my house and drinking does not appeal, and I think it's a subconscious reaction from that time when it's all I ever did. To me, it feels messy, and if you're trying to mend your life and make it better, the last thing you need to do is go backwards. I don't want to be hitting my forties with that. It's all been a huge learning process for me, but it takes a lot of mental discipline to keep all those spiky things under control. I try not to let myself get too depressed, too excited or too stressed. Of course, everyone has ups and downs, but I am always mindful of keeping the highs, the lows and my anxiety at a manageable level. It's a delicate balance and not getting out of control with alcohol or anything else is a big part of that.

Some would say my life is comfortable and perhaps a bit boring away from the band, but that's how I like it. I enjoy my own company, and I enjoy sleep. God, I've never slept so much in my life. There are so many lovely things I have because I'm living differently. My only sadness is that I'm fuzzy on so much of my past. I wish I had more clarity on some of what has passed. At the time of writing this, I've just turned forty, but let's not forget, I started young. I've done enough partying for a couple of lifetimes.

My family ties are still as strong as ever, and in many ways more important than they have ever been. Along with my closest friends, they have been my backbone. I owe my mum and dad everything. And let's not forget Tahlia. It's a cliché, but having her was the best gift I could ask for. In many ways, she saved me, and I love her with every breath I take.

Over the last few years I've started to notice my parents getting older. It's the kind of thing that creeps up on you. I feel blessed to have had them with me for so many years with all that's happened, and it's good to see that, despite everything, they're still going strong.

My dad is and always has been a walking warrior. Now in his late seventies, he's still very strong, with long black hair down past his shoulders – only recently has the grey crept in. He's aged so well, and looking at him even now, you'd never be able to guess his age. Sometimes, I can see he's got aches and pains, but he's not a person to sit there complaining about it. I love him for having that strength.

Now in my forties, I've started to think properly about taking care of myself. Cancer is something that runs in my family: we've had quite a few family members who have passed away from various forms of the disease. This fact has opened my eyes to what can happen and made me realize the importance of self-care and health. There are many things I didn't care about before that I now try to consider – what I eat and put into my body and the products I use on my skin and around the house. I try to stay away from things that are not good for me in all senses of the word.

The older we get, the more things crop up over time. Life events happen, some good, some bad. You just have to roll with it and let it remind you to appreciate the people that you love. You've got to hold them close. My mum is still the amazing woman she always has been. She raised eight kids and even more grandkids, and has never failed us.

It's strange to think that there were times when I needed my family in my life but was afraid to turn to them, whether it was my brothers when I was in relationships with abusive or violent men, or my sisters when I was in despair, feeling lost and harming myself. I think if those things were happening now, I would be much more inclined to lean on family, which, I suppose, is how it should be. The difference now is that I'm looking at my life with a sensible head, clear of all the things that led me to bad choices.

My sisters and I talk all the time. Most mornings, we'll end up on a group phone call. We're all early risers, so it's inevitable. Mostly, it'll be my little sister Dalisay, who never has anything specific to discuss; she just wants to yap. It doesn't matter how busy any of us are; if she wants to chat, we chat.

Ligaya has three kids, a daughter named Mayana, a little boy, Datu, and stepson Jaxson. Dalisay also has a daughter, Tiara-loves. Of course, with all my nieces and nephews I'm confident I'm the favourite auntie. They might not have all said it out loud; I just know it. There are nineteen nieces and nephews altogether and our family gatherings are as rowdy as ever.

As a family, we will always find an excuse to meet. We don't need a birthday, anniversary or special occasion; we love being in one another's company and hanging out together. If the sun's out, be sure we're having a barbecue.

In January 2025, after some Sugababes gigs in Australia, I flew to the Philippines for a couple of weeks of much-needed holiday. While I was there, some of my family from London flew over, including Tahlia. Mum and Dad were already there. We stayed at our family home in Bohol, and it was there I realized that, one day, my life would be in the Philippines. I always feel so free there, and everything about it makes me feel like I'm home. During my stay, I saw all my extended family and travelled the beautiful islands, realizing there's still so much more I need to see. For now, though, I'll keep working until I'm ready to go on that journey, and continue enjoying my new home in the UK.

Finally being able to buy my own place again has been a big and important step for me after everything that's happened. I'd never been the greatest of savers, so going from bankruptcy to having enough money to invest in a property I love without compromise is a beautiful thing. It came as a bit of a shock, the idea that I'd learned how to save, especially when I thought about how much I'd squandered back in the day, paying for drinks and cabs for everyone on a thousand nights out, and never really considering the future.

Gradually, through all the shows we were doing, plus a few royalties and money coming in from past ventures, I was able to build things back up again to the point where I felt secure for the first time in years.

My new place is beautiful. It's in a quiet village and even has a pool at the back. I finally got the keys last summer, and it felt great. Of course, all my nephews and nieces were dying to come around to see Auntie's new place, so on a hot sunny day at the end of July, they all came over with their swimming costumes. There wasn't a stick of furniture in the place, but we ordered pizza and all jumped in the pool. I always love seeing the smiles on their faces when they're playing in the water. The kids in our family are all water babies, and I'd made it a tradition on my birthday every year to rent a house with a pool for us to enjoy. Now I had a house all of my own.

It's great that Mum and Dad can get out of London and come stay with me whenever they feel like it. Seeing them sipping their teas and coffees in the bright conservatory or around the pool makes me happy. It's exactly what I'd wanted in a home: a place that I loved but that my nearest and dearest could enjoy too.

The only slight downside is that for Tahlia it's too quiet and remote. She wants to stay a bit closer to London, so at the moment she's in the midst of deciding whether she wants to live with her dad or me, and whatever she decides is fine. She's nineteen, turning twenty, and when I was her age I wanted to be in the thick of it all. In truth, my house is only about half an hour from London, but the beautiful road it's on is mostly inhabited by older people. It's a quiet place and I'm probably going to be the one disturbing the peace!

She wants to enrol in college to study audio technology to become a sound engineer. At the moment, she sometimes shadows our sound and production man, Chris, for work experience. I think she'd make a great tour or production manager, and I'm happy she's got a vocation in life that I might be able to help with. It's nice to know she has options on all these things. As things turned out, having Tahlia at such a young age was a blessing in many ways. Having only twenty years between us has been such a good thing. We celebrate so much together, go on holidays together, and if I fancy a night out, she's now of the age that I can bring her along with me. She's not too young, and I'm not too old!

The best part about buying the house has been the reaction of my family and closest friends, all telling me how proud they are of me for coming so far. It has been a journey for sure. It's taken me a long time to get back to the place I once was financially, and to feel like I'm deserving of that security. I've started afresh, with new beds, sofas and chairs; I think it's important that's it's all brand new, with fresh, positive energy.

It really is in the middle of nowhere, which suits me. I don't plan on leaving the house much unless I'm working. These days, I love keeping myself to myself when I'm home. I don't even plan on having a lot of people over apart from the family, which is the opposite of how things were in the past.

And no, I'm not missing out on anything. I've already done it all.

Acknowledgements

FIRST, I REALLY WANT TO thank God for keeping me safe – you have always been there whenever I've needed you, from my lowest to my highest. I give thanks to you.

A big thank you to my mama and papa for having me (lol) and for being there and loving me always. I absolutely love you both for eternity. I've been through so much shit and you've never failed to be there for me, and for Tyty, having my back throughout the years.

THANK YOU to my brothers and sisters – my biggest supporters – for putting up with me; the older we get, the more I just want to be near you. I love you dearly. Also, my extended sisters Anika and Carrie-Anne – thank you to both of you. I love you. Now my nieces and nephews – so many to mention – but God knows I'm so proud of each and every one of you. You're all beautiful and handsome and I thank you for being in my life. Big kisses and love to my auntie Jackie, who kept getting me those gigs, and was always there for me.

A big thank you to my besties, Latoya (wifey), Anupa, Nicki, Melissa, Natania (baby-mama), Dan Dan (Hazelwood), Zaza, Danni, Dean, Charlie. I absolutely love you – you're always there when I need you, especially when it comes to partying or coming to work with me! I love all my godchildren, you know who you are. I'm blessed to have you in my life.

I want to say a big thank you to my sugar ladies: Keisha, who's been my sister from the age of eight, I can't express how much I love you and I'm so proud that we're here together, able to live this life, singing and travelling the world. I look forward to going on until we're old and grey. Siobhan, I've also known you for a very long time and I love you and the sisterhood we all have. You and Keisha are so talented, I adore both of you.

While I'm here, a shout out to Mr Devon and Miss Ro-Ro for always making me look absolutely beautiful in our shows. I've known both of you for a very long time too, so it's important for me to say thank you for being a part of my life and my journey.

I'm going to save the best to last, and that is to thank my darling beautiful daughter, Tahlia. Without you in my life, I would probably be a hot mess, and I have loved watching you grow up into a beautiful woman. It's always been me and you, and it always will till the day I die. I have so much love, time and respect for you, always – even though sometimes we may bang heads with one another (who doesn't with their children?!) – I love you more than words can explain, more than my life itself. I'm proud to be your mama.

One last thing: I want to say a massive thank you to all my fans who have been there for me since day one, who have never left me and have supported everything I have done – past, present and future. I love you guys and I want to keep making magic for everyone to enjoy.

Picture Acknowledgements

All photographs in the picture section have been kindly supplied by the author, except those listed below.

Page 5, top
Dave Hogan

Page 5, bottom
Dave Tonge

Page 6, top
Gareth Cattermole

Page 6, bottom
Rune Hellestad – Corbis

Page 8, top
JMEnternational

Page 8, bottom
Dave Benett

About the Author

Mutya Buena is an English singer and songwriter who rose to fame as a member of girl group Sugababes. With Sugababes, Mutya had four UK number-one singles, an additional six top-ten hits and three multi-platinum albums. After leaving the group in December 2005, she released her debut solo album, *Real Girl*, in June 2007. Mutya returned to Sugababes with the original line-up in 2012.